This Jove book contains the complete
text of the original hardcover edition.
It has been completely reset in a typeface
designed for easy reading and was
printed from new film.

THE PIMLICO PLOT

A Jove Book / published by arrangement with
the author

PRINTING HISTORY
Doubleday & Company edition published 1975
Jove edition / June 1988

ISBN: 0-515-09544-3

Jove Books are published by The Berkley Publishing Group,
200 Madison Avenue, New York, New York 10016.
The name "JOVE" and the "J" logo
are trademarks belonging to Jove Publications, Inc.

PRINTED IN THE UNITED STATES OF AMERICA

10 9 8 7 6 5 4 3 2 1

The Demon Lover

Fen was, she hoped and believed, deeply asleep when the footsteps went by, and the soft whistling rose on the night air.

"The Young May Moon" . . .

Over the sudden pounding of her heart, she listened to the crisp long-striding lilt of the footsteps, the faint ring of metaled heels. She had waited with longing to hear the sound, so many, many times.

A phrase from the song floated intrusively through her mind: ". . . and the best of all ways to lengthen our days/Is to steal a few hours from the night, my dear. . . ."

A pause, before 11 Polperry Mews, and then the feet went leisurely on. Tense, sweating, she lay listening, seeing in her mind's eye night-wandering, whistling Desmond and his companion, a man from the sound of it, going down the mews . . .

THE PIMLICO
MARY McMUL

JOVE BOOKS, NEW YORK

To Alton

THE PIMLICO PLOT

PART
ONE

ONE

Peacefully unaware that she was in the process of making the most important decision of her life—the party or not the party, surely a thistledown question?—Maeve Devlin finished her designer's sketch of a little girl's suit, in peacock-blue Moygashel linen. The cut of the brass-buttoned square jacket was tactful about the round young stomach that would disappear a little after the age of five. She started on the small boy's matching suit.

It was a Saturday afternoon in New York in March, dark, with rain and sleet coming down. Her drawing board was at the far end of the bedroom, near the window. She was working because she enjoyed it, not because she was behind at her office. It was warm here, brightly lit and quiet. Why leave this at five o'clock, leave the fire she would light, the book, the music, the soft cushiony corner of the sofa, and for what?

A roomful of chattering strangers, trying to find things to say to each other to cover that forbidden thing, silence. Have

3

you read, have you seen, have you been to—have you heard
about. . . ?

And then while John Lee, who had asked her to the party
with him, went to get her another drink, some cruising bore
would spot her. Mistaking her natural politeness for interest,
he would discourse to her on professional football, or the state
of the market, or the latest sex manual.

John, a restless butterfly of a man, seeing that she was safely
taken care of, might well go and join the group emitting the
highest decibels of talk and laughter.

His own girl, he said, couldn't make it. Please come, Maeve.
She, their hostess, was sinfully rich, and there would be quan-
tities of caviar. He said he had his image to think about and
must arrive with some sort of marvelous girl at his side.

She stapled a swatch of the blue Moygashel linen to the
corner of her *croquis*. The dark and the cold outside produced
a sudden vision of Desmond, watching her at her work, standing
behind her, in the tall white room in Dublin, with his hand on
her shoulder. Desmond, as usual having appeared from nowhere
and walking confidently back into her life.

"I hope," he had said, with a tightening of his hand, "that
you don't do that work of yours out of a sort of vicarious
motherliness?"

She considered this and said, "I don't think so, it's just more
fun than the ladies', and in any case why do you ask?"

"I don't want to have children, when and if I marry."

"Or," Maeve went on thoughtfully, "I suppose I could still
just be dressing my dolls, but I don't think so . . . your intentions
about your progeny or lack of them are no concern of mine,
Desmond."

He laughed and bent and kissed her hair.

"That's what you think."

And she felt again, as she had often felt during the last year
or so, some faint emanation coming from him, of darkness, or
danger, she couldn't put an exact word to it; she moved lightly
but decisively away from his hand.

The wind changed direction and hurled sleet attackingly at
the window. That one savage gust made up her mind. She went
to the telephone and called John Lee and said, yes, after all,
she'd like to go to the party with him. Perhaps, this once, no
one would talk to her about professional football.

*   *   *

He was standing, momentarily alone, in a corner about fifteen feet away. Picking up bits and pieces of party noises woven through John's animated voice, she was vaguely aware that their hostess, Mrs. Something Betterly, had just moved, archly laughing, away from the corner. Or been gotten rid of.

It was his eyes, on her, that she was first aware of, causing her to turn her head to discover whose gaze was making this mysterious impact.

He was tall, and very straight, an easy but notable sort of carriage. He had a thoughtful, formally boned face with intelligent witty planes and angles to it. She wasn't sure what color his eyes were under the brows, very strongly marked and dark, as his hair was over the fine forehead. Gray, or blue, or both.

Their eyes locked, and held.

". . . and she told him five thousand more *and* a vice-presidency, or get out of my bed for good," John was saying. "I mean, you've got to hand it to her . . ."

His voice seemed to come from very far away.

How long had they been looking at each other? Fifteen seconds, thirty? A full minute? She must force herself to look away. This was indecent. Certainly, he was a man to be stared at. In any room, in any company, he would be remarkable. But then, she wasn't exactly staring. And his gaze couldn't be called a stare either; it was a good deal more personal than that.

He moved suddenly, and started toward her, going steadily around and through the standing, laughing pack of grouped bodies. His eyes were still on her. Oh God, it's just that I'm here near the door and he's bored and he's leaving and I'll never even know who he is, she thought with a stab of something very like genuine woe.

He was three feet away; now two. She felt as if she was drowning in the searchlight gaze.

He put out a strong and shapely hand and closed it casually over her bare forearm. John, not having reached the end of his story but aware of being joined, went on, "Oh, hi, and he said to her—"

"I'm sorry," the tall man said, firmly interrupting, addressing himself to John. "Would you mind if I borrowed her for a bit? We've very old friends and we haven't seen each other for a long time. I must have a minute with her—"

John raised his eyebrows and opened his mouth to say something but she had already been detached from his side. She was led very quickly back through the bodies, through a far door and across a stretch of Kirman carpet into another room, a library it looked to be, with nobody in it at all. His closing of the door shut off the tide of rhythmic, wavelike sound.

He came back to where she stood in the center of the room. He looked down at her and said, "Who are you?"

"Apart from being an old friend of yours, do you mean?" She smiled faintly.

"You're right, this is a little abrupt, but I thought you might take a look around you and cut and run, as I was about to do, when— Or, I might have been caught up with some frightful group at any moment and you'd have vanished while my back was turned."

"I'm Maeve Devlin. And who are you?"

"Fenway—Fen—Vaughan."

"You couldn't be. That's a publishing house, and there's an ampersand in between the Fenway and the Vaughan."

"Simple. Mr. Fenway's daughter married Mr. Vaughan's son. I am one of the products of that alliance. And you—you don't look or sound like the standard American model stamped out in Detroit."

"I am a product of aunts."

"A biological first, but clearly a success."

He was waiting; she wanted, for some reason, to tell him more about herself.

"My parents died when I was an infant. I grew up spending the school year with my Dublin aunt, my mother's sister, in Ireland, and the summer vacations with my New York aunt, my father's sister. I'm an American citizen but something of a hybrid, as you can see."

"As I can see." The intent eyes, moving about her face and head and throat, made her not at all uncomfortable; but warmed her.

She was slender and a little above medium height, with a narrow, sensitively modeled face. The soft, floaty hair, of a shining dark, chestnut red in the low light, was center-parted and lifted itself over the quiet fair brow, curved in loosely against her cheeks, and fell almost to her shoulders. Her eyes were a mossy green color, aware and responsive and well able to speak. Her mouth had tender corners.

She had, he told her later, a very private kind of beauty. "You don't come on like a full orchestra but like a faraway sound that's quite lovely, you don't know what it is but you want to hear more of it. . . ."

He had a good voice, rounded, vibrant. For the first time since he had led her into the little library room, it took on a slight edge of uncertainty.

"That man you're with . . . ?"

"Yes, I'll have to get back to him in a few moments, I'm being rude . . . very nice, but no one in particular. I'm filling in for his girl, she has the flu."

He laughed. "*You*, filling in! How did you know about Fenway and Vaughan, with the ampersand?"

"Their, or your, building is right around the corner from my apartment. I pass it every day on my way to work. And I do occasionally open a book, in fact it's rather a fault of mine."

"You mean—" He looked stunned. "You mean you have been going by that building for—how long? And I never even saw you? Maybe never would have seen you at all, except for this party, which I almost didn't come to?"

"And I almost didn't, either . . . two years, going past your building . . ."

She found herself very much aware—although he had not touched her since he had brought her here—of the taut fine body, broad-shouldered, deep-chested, under the polite coverings. The suit, very dark gray, London, probably. The blue and white striped shirt with its immaculate white collar, the elegant jut of the Windsor knot of the blue tie under the strong classic line of the jaw.

"Not really my building any more, perhaps a couple of rooms of it, I'm an editor there. What do you do for your living, if anything?"

"Design children's clothes. And one of the reasons we may not have encountered each other at your doorstep is that I still spend a lot of time in Ireland."

"I trust you're not on the brink of another departure?"

"No—except back to the living room, I really must—"

He took her hand and held it coolly and loosely. "Will you have dinner with me—I won't be in town tomorrow—Monday night?"

"Yes. I might be held up a bit, a meeting late in the day—"

"It doesn't matter. Let me have your number there, and at home, and here's mine, for you. You don't play by the regular rules, do you? 'How nice of you to ask me to dinner, of course

I'd like to, but this coming week is bad, perhaps if you'll give me a ring sometime in the middle of the week after' . . . ?''

"No, I do not," Maeve said, and something about her intonation made him smile.

"Now I'll return you temporarily to your man out there and take myself off. Good night, Maeve."

"Good night, Fen." A nice word to taste in her mouth.

John Lee watched her face with normal, vague male jealousy while she watched Fen Vaughan saying what were obviously his thank you's and good night's to Mrs. Betterly.

"Vaughan? . . . You've never mentioned him before. Is his wife here? I assume he's married. Women don't let men who look that good walk around unspoken for."

She realized that the thought had never even crossed her mind, and that she had no idea whether he was married or not. She felt suddenly deflated, back from under a sort of spell—a feeling that something of importance might have happened, or started to happen, in the library—and into an atmosphere too hot, hazed with smoke, jaggedly noisy.

Fen Vaughan lifted a hand to her from across the room and disappeared into the entrance hall.

"Get me one last quick drink, will you, John?" She just remembered in time that they were supposed to be old friends. "Married . . . ? I'd suppose so. It never occurred to me to ask him, to tell you the truth."

The flowers arrived at 8:30 Sunday morning. Lovely to see them, sniff them, with the March storm whirling outside. The sleet and rain had turned to snow sometime during the night.

There were lilies of the valley, and white freesias, white lilacs, and glossy white tulips. The card, in a decided and stylish hand, said, "Good morning, Maeve. Fen."

The telephone rang as she was putting the flowers in a mercury-glass pitcher.

"Did I wake you?"

"No, my nose was buried in your delightful flowers, thank you very much." She hesitated. In a way, it was an awkward question she wanted to put to him; it would imply that the eyes and the silences, the flowers and the dinner invitation, meant some formal intention of sorts.

But she had had enough of painful ambiguities in her life, with men. Get on with it.

"I have to ask you something that sounds most abrupt, and not at all contemporary. Are you married?" Nothing anxious about her tone; it was interested and direct.

There was a pause that couldn't have lasted more than a few seconds but seemed to go on forever.

"Yes, my wife is right here in bed beside me, she likes to share my morning chats with my girls." She didn't know his voice that well, but she sensed in it a certain surprise and a slight anger. Then: "Of course not. I was. Let me ask you an uncontemporary question. Are you? I'm not sure why, but I didn't think—"

"No."

"Go back to your breakfast, then. I'll see you tomorrow night which seems, from here, roughly forever. You have a pretty voice, Maeve."

It was the voice that was to say to him, steadily, out of an aching throat, several months in the future, "Well, you walked up to your fate and chose it, didn't you?"

T W O

"I can't imagine you at a meeting, for some reason," Fen said.
"You look more as if you belong wandering about on a tapestry
up at the Cloisters, with a unicorn for company. Do you say
things like, 'I'd like to speak to that point,' and 'Is this truly
relevant?' and 'Let's keep our options open'?"

"No. I mostly shut up and think about other things, real
things, today, you, as a matter of fact. Or I take refuge and
scribble collars and sleeves on my pad. I notice you don't use
any of that rubble language, either, or not so far."

"I refuse to go around wearing a uniform of current words."

She had wondered for two days if Saturday night wasn't just
a ridiculous bit of fireworks brought on by some strange mood
of his and if this would be just a nice evening with a nice man
who had taken a fancy to seeing her once again at least.

Coming into the small, good French restaurant on Third
Avenue, after eight o'clock, tired and a little cross from having
been kept so long at a ponderous meeting about almost nothing,

10

she saw him standing alone at the bar, near the door, his back to it, watching, waiting; he took the door from her hand and opened it wider, intercepting the proprietor, and caught her other hand.

A wave of feeling swept her from head to foot; fatigue fell away. She smiled at him.

"I'm sorry I'm so late—how many drinks ahead of me are you?"

"One. We'll catch up."

It hadn't been any trick of low light and deep shadow in Mrs. Betterly's library. She studied his face with great pleasure, and felt the pleasure returned.

They had a drink at the bar and another at the small table where the banquette made a corner and they sat at close right angles to each other.

She told him about her agreeable open-ended job; as long as she did her four series of seasonal designs a year, she was more or less free to come and go as she pleased. Besides being able to join her other self in Ireland, she said, she found a lot of her fabrics there and had a good deal of her handwork done, smocking and laces and embroidery.

"It helps that my employer is a friend of my Aunt Brenda's, if you can imagine an Irish garment manufacturer. I don't make a lot of money in your—in American terms, but the freedom is worth it."

He told her about Fenway and Vaughan, owned now by one of the giant publishing houses but still retaining a crisp identity. She listened to his stories about the writers on his list with fascinated amusement, and thought, Thank God you can speak English, thank God you're not a bore. They fell into an amiable half-argument about books they liked, writers they did or didn't like. They ate smoked salmon, grilled sole, an endive salad, fresh pears and Camembert, and drank Chablis.

There were little stirrings, under the surface, where the flesh and blood was, during the civilized exchange of voices.

"Why do you keep looking at my hands?"

"I had rather a strong dose of your eyes the other night, and this close, they're—but they are, your hands, well made."

"I'm glad to hear you express an interest in them."

With their demitasse: "Tomorrow night, of course?"

"I have something to do but I'll cancel it."

"I did the same thing while I was waiting for you."

Wonderingly, she said, "I'm not quite sure I know what this is all about."

"You know perfectly well what this is all about."

She did meet his eyes, now. They were very steady and very grave and then a kind of merriment came over them.

He placed his hands on the table in front of her.

"Don't worry, Maeve, you'll be quite safe in these."

They had a nightcap in a small dark bar where a woman sang sadly and sexily in French, and then he took her home.

She lived in a brownstone on Murray Hill, between Lexington and Third. They climbed the graceful flight of stairs past the parlor floor and came to her landing on the second floor.

"You don't look it but you must be tired."

He put his fingers lightly on her shoulders and stood looking down at her. He bent his head. He moved the surface of his lips very delicately, featheringly, over the texture of hers; then he tightened his fingers and kissed her at first gently and again with force. His hands fell suddenly away and he took a quick startled step backward.

"Well, I—" She was not ordinarily a fumbler but she was having considerable difficulty with her keys. She found the right one. Her hand was faintly trembling. He closed his hand over it, guided the key into the lock, gave the paired hands a firm twist to the right, and pushed the unlocked door inward.

Then he said, "I'll call you in the morning," and before she was well through her doorway she heard his running footsteps on the stairs.

"Do you always bid your girls good night so abruptly, Fen?" she asked him over the telephone, after it rang at eight o'clock in the morning.

"Not as an ordinary thing, no," he said. "But with you, last night, I was just about two minutes away from statutory rape."

"What did you cancel for this?" she asked, over her chicken hash. They were at a quiet restaurant near the United Nations building. Piano music sparkled discreetly. Candlelight mused over Fen's cheekbones and thoughtful, good mouth. She wore a dress of an unreal smoke blue, with handkerchiefs of the chiffon floating from the shoulders and the waist. No late meeting tonight; there had been time for a bath and fresh perfume and very light new makeup. Her skin was so fair that in the candlelight, and perhaps reflecting her chiffon, it looked faintly and mysteriously blue.

"A dinner party."

"Business or pleasure or both?"

"Both. Heather Appleby, over from London." One of his writers; Maeve had read her, a woman of rather mystic dry wit whose books were composed almost solely of dialogue.

She ate a forkful of hash and said severely, "You mustn't neglect your work for me."

"No, and I promise to brush my teeth before I go to bed, Mother," Fen said. "What did you cancel for this?"

"Just a man."

"If I ever thought you would describe me, to another man, as just a man, I would jump into an open elevator shaft."

"I wouldn't," she promised lightly, "any more than I'd say Monet is just a painter . . . and he'll already have filled the slot with another girl."

She lifted her glass and tasted her wine and said, "Speaking of other girls . . . you said when I asked you if you were married, 'I was.' "

"She died," he said. "Four years ago. In a little private plane of some friends', going up to Nantucket. I was to join them the next day—"

She was silent. He wasn't looking at her, but downward and inward; she saw the black of the lowered lashes over the cheek-bones. She felt that for the moment there was nothing at all to say; you didn't murmur, "I'm sorry," as over a shattered glass or a lost wallet. Happy marriage? Probably, she thought. There was nothing haunted, unfinished, about the expression on his face when he came back to her from wherever he had been.

"I didn't mean to pry—may I have some bread?"

"You may have the whole loaf if you like. I enjoy your appetite, Maeve, among other things. For a blue ghost, you consume an impressive amount of food."

When he took her home she said at the door, "Come in for a drink if you'd like to."

"I'd like to very much."

She saw him scanning intently the pleasant room, her personal landscape, the high ceilings and watery mirrors, the shelves of books, some good furniture from her family past mingling comfortably with airy white wicker, the pictures and prints on the walls. Inevitably, he went over to study her taste in books, took out a very beautiful *Alice in Wonderland* bound in currant-red leather soft as satin, handling it with a delicate affection.

"Where did you find this?"

"An auction, somewhere on Fifty-sixth Street . . . will you fix our drinks, please?"

He went to the teacart between the two tall windows. He seemed perfectly at ease; but then, she thought that to him she would seem so, too, and she wasn't, not at all. The quiet worried her; she flicked on the phonograph and Mozart immediately silvered the air.

Handing her her scotch, Fen said with a smile, "I like the climate you live in."

He sat on her down-cushioned sofa and she sat on the wicker chair on the other side of the coffee table, facing him. They talked, carefully and composedly, about politics, on which they found themselves to be of one mind, and the play they had seen before they dined, and the work of Heather Appleby.

Fen, who had obviously been stretching his drink, finished it and put the glass down on the warm apricot-veined white marble of the table.

He said, "This isn't, after all, a tea party in Dublin."

He got up from the sofa. She saw his elegant tall carriage outlined with lamplight. He came over to her, bent down, and took her hand.

"Let me escort you, to me."

"I've been waiting for an invitation . . . I hardly liked to dash myself down beside you the minute we came in and say, Here I am, Fen Vaughan—"

Whatever else she had to say was stopped, under his mouth. After a time in each other's arms, while they kissed, slowly, savoringly, he linked his fingers through hers and took her to the sofa and arranged her beside him in the circle of his arm.

She looked deep into the eyes four inches away.

"Well, then, here I am, Fen Vaughan."

"And here I am, Maeve Devlin."

He added thoughtfully, "I hate to crush that lovely dress."

"It doesn't matter, but it doesn't crush. . . ."

The Mozart record dropped itself and the sound of vintage jazz piano, largely unheard, rose to the high white plaster-garlanded ceiling, and fell gaily about the room.

"I believe you said I was safe in your hands?"

He lifted his head and smiled down at her. "You are as safe with me, at any time, as you would like to be."

"That's an interesting answer—"

When the jazz piano record clicked down, into silence, he took her left hand and regarded her bare ring finger.

"Tell me about this. You're twenty-nine, you said."

"Shall we have another drink? I'm a bit dizzy, I need sobering up."

While he made the drinks, she said, "When I was at the age when most girls marry, I was involved in complications I'd be much happier not to go into, at least at the moment. The field has necessarily narrowed now, most of the attractive men have made their arrangements. And I'm not right for the suburban life that's been offered to me on occasion, there's nothing wrong with it except me. I wouldn't fit. John Cheever—I like to read him but I couldn't live it. Perhaps I've been spoiled, with my two worlds. When you tire of one, you can run to the other and start all fresh again. . . ."

He gave her a long look. "And you really mean to tell me there isn't a man I have to worry about?"

"Not just at this instant, Fen."

The telephone made a sudden commotion on the table at the end of the sofa.

It was close to one o'clock. He watched her as she got up and reluctantly picked up the receiver. When, after listening for a moment to the deep male voice which made itself heard in strong salutation, she said, "What, six o'clock in the morning, are you up to your knees in Guinness . . . ?" he felt compelled to give her privacy, tried the kitchen, found it was no good as it hadn't a door, pushed open another door and went into her bedroom and firmly closed himself in.

A nice room, as large as the living room, with its drawing board and colorful cluttered white desk at the window end and its bed covered with rough white Irish lace over a heavy blue linen petticoat. The air smelt of her. His flowers, still in pristine condition, were on the table beside the bed.

"What are you sounding guarded for?" Desmond Byrne demanded. "Do you have someone there?"

"Yes, I have."

"Dressed or undressed?"

"Desmond, I—" She forced patience on herself. "Go to bed,

for God's sake. It's never easy to tell, but I think you're drunk. You'll ruin your health."

"Actually it doesn't matter who's there, and if he has his clothes on or off, as long as you remember, whether you like it or not and whether you want it or not, that you are mine."

THREE

"As I was saying," Fen said, "do you really mean to tell me there isn't a man? From Ireland, I gather—you said six o'clock in the morning. Your other world. You sounded a bit like a scolding wife."

"Let's go back to my more or less maiden state. There isn't a man I want to marry."

"You're being a little evasive. It isn't like you, or what I know of you. Up till now I thought you were the most direct woman I've ever met. . . . Am I faced with some fatal passion?"

He asked it lightly. His eyes were deadly in earnest, darker. He didn't sit down again, but stood, with his glass in his hand, a foot away from her. To his ears, the words erupting from the telephone still faintly reverberated on the air: *"Maeve love . . ."*

"Someone, say, who won't divorce his wife for you?" His voice was puzzled, and wary, a note she had never heard in it before.

"No, to both." She had every reason, at the time, to believe she was speaking the exact truth.

He studied her, then put down his drink and took her in his arms. "We'll leave it for now but—I seldom set foot in the suburbs, I do like the country in small doses but I'm afraid I'm a hopeless city dweller, good night, my darling, I'd better go, you'd better remove yourself, immediately—"

"How can I? I'm trapped. Your arms—"

Mouth to mouth, they took breath to laugh, and then he turned away a little blindly and walked the length of the room and opened the door and was gone.

A week later, she said to him, "As things go these days— hello, you look all right, let's get to bed—you went about it all very gracefully and deliberately, Fen. Why? I almost ran after you that night and said, 'Don't leave me, you mustn't.' . . . "

"I wanted to go very slowly up your street," he told her. "I wanted to see all the views, I didn't want to miss anything, the brook or the apple orchard. I wanted to hear your birds and smell your flowers. It seemed far too important for rushing, and grabbing . . . and I knew from the first what it was going to end in, anyway."

He had to leave, the next morning, for San Francisco, where a conference would keep him for three days. Maeve went about her work, feeling halved, lost, and in the better hours happier than she had ever been in her life.

He called her before she was out of bed in the morning, and while she was at work, and in the evening, late; she said no to everybody who asked her out.

"You're a frightfully extravagant man," she said. "At *your* meetings, do you talk about keeping your options open, and what the overview is, and 'I'd like to speak to that point'?"

"No, I mostly shut up and think about you." He paused a moment. "Has your Guinness friend been calling you too?"

"Have you been brooding about him?"

"Not brooding. I'm curious, though, very. The more I think about it the less he sounds like a cousin, or a friend, or your . . . just a man."

"Now that you mention it, he is a sort of cousin, I suppose." Carelessly and gaily, she added, "You shall know all about him if you like, right down to the exact color and count of his eyelashes."

"Thanks," Fen said, "but you can keep that piece of information to yourself."

The jet, on his return flight, was over Chicago when she unwillingly boarded a plane for Boston. Angela Lane, publicity director for Storyland, Inc., had fallen ill and there was a children's fashion show to be organized and run at Filene's.

Somehow, the impossible noisy tangle of small boys and girls was smoothed, rehearsed, timed. She stayed at the Ritz, in mild revenge against Liam Cochran, Storyland's president, who had gotten her into this morass, and the next afternoon did the show, acting as narrator and sash-tier and occasional lightning disciplinarian.

. . . Fen, what are you doing now, right this minute?

Five whole days without him. Perhaps, by now, he might have cooled. Three thousand miles gives a certain perspective. Watch yourself, Fen, he might think. Look before you leap. . . .

She was describing an apricot batiste party dress, smocked, tied at the shoulders with narrow pale blue velvet ribbons which floated to the hem front and back, when she saw, in the polite young Boston audience to the right of the runway, Desmond's friend Cooley.

He sat, awkward in his height and thinness, on the small gilt chair. He grinned at her when her glance met his. He was very dark, with a long narrow face hitched by some flaw in his jawbone a bit to one side. An unlikely presence here, watching the parading children; an unlikely man in any case. Daniel Cooley, traveler in laces and trimmings, Mahoney Brothers, Dublin. At least, as a cover job.

He looked more like someone you would come upon at the opening of a dark alley, and you would pick up your feet and hurry on, fast, trying not to steal a glance behind you.

No reason why, coincidentally, he shouldn't be here. He must be peddling his laces and trimmings to the notions buyer. And there was a good deal of Irish wealth in Boston, if in addition to his laces he was following his other pursuit.

The show over, he came up to her and said, "Hello, Maeve, what about a drink?"

She was not on terms with him that could remotely have been described as social, and found the invitation and his sly repeated grin offensive. I do not drink, Mr. Cooley, with the

people who surface out of the darkness of Desmond's other
world.

"Can't, sorry . . . Oh, hello, Mr. Fernald . . ." She turned
away from him to the buyer of children's clothing, a round
rosy man with an invitation that could not conscientiously be
turned down, to drinks and dinner. Out of the corner of her
eye, she saw Cooley move away with a backward glance and
a shrug.

Dinner was long and late. Fen's face kept imposing itself
over the kind pink one across the table, and she heard his voice
through her nerve ends. Here I am, Maeve Devlin. . . .

Cooley was on the plane, going back. She was thankful that
the two seats beside her were occupied. She sat on the aisle
and was startled to feel the hand on her shoulder, see the dark
thin shape bending over her.

"No chance to talk, back there, business is business, isn't
that the truth?" He poked a passing stewardess in the small of
the back. "A drink for this lady, miss."

She refused it and he pressed it on her, to the gathering
interest of drowsing passengers.

"Desmond told me to look you up, see how you are, take
your pulse, you might say, give him the word on you, and here
by good fortune we are on the very same aircraft."

He lounged over her, leaning against the seat in front, an
oppressive presence. She looked up into his sideways-hitched
face, with its soiled-colored skin and uneasy small dark eyes,
and said, "I have some work to catch up on, if you'll excuse
me."

"Oh, I wouldn't want to interfere with that—" He saluted
her with his own drink, inevitably said, *"Slainte!"* and with
his elbow almost knocked the Boston hat from the head of the
woman in front of her. A glare, a hiss, a "Would you mind
removing yourself, if you must have a party can't you have it
at the back of the plane?"

Unruffled, Cooley said, "I'll tell him you're blooming. Absolutely blooming. When we get to New York, I'll drive you
home. I have a car at Kennedy—"

"Thanks, I'm being met." She handed him her untasted drink.
"You'd better have this, I don't want it. Good night, Mr.
Cooley."

With a sullen, slapped look, he moved away.

It was after one o'clock when she let herself into her apartment. She had called Fen from Boston and said she would be home very late. There was silence from the telephone as she undressed and went to bed.

Silence again, in the morning. Perhaps he thought she would be sleeping late and didn't want to wake her. How, think back, had he sounded last evening? Nice, eager to see her. A bit abstracted—worried about somebody's manuscript . . . ?

It was one of those days in New York that said, Don't give up, spring is coming, it really is. The air was soft and balmy, the sky a high and polished blue.

As always, she turned the corner and walked past Fenway & Vaughan, Incorporated, on her way to work. A handsome building, occupying a space the width of two town houses. Classic limestone blocks, Ionic columns on either side of the linenfold-carved English oak door, a graceful pediment, three thriving young ginkgo trees at intervals along the sidewalk in front of it. She paused and looked up. It was well after ten o'clock. He usually, he had told her, got there at 9:30.

She resumed her fast easy walk. The street was almost empty, everybody but herself toeing the line, busily at work.

There was a step behind her. A dark blue arm went around her waist and a mouth kissed her on the nape of the neck.

"I saw you standing there, looking up," he said. "The elevator was stuck and I almost broke a leg running down three flights of stairs—"

She was breathless, stunned at the surge of emotion that broke over her, excitement and wonder and joy.

Under a maple tree moving its faintly budding branches in the warm wind, he examined her minutely, almost anxiously. "Well, your eyes are still green, and your hair is still chestnut or titian or both . . . Einstein had a point, you know, about time. It was the longest five days of my life."

"You look like you, too, but younger, in a way . . ."

"I always look younger when I'm worried about something."

"Worried about what?"

"That you'd go up in smoke, or leave for Dublin, or re-list me as, just a man, thinking things over in the cold light of Copley Square—"

"And I was worried too, distance lending disenchantment, who is this bloody woman anyway, we Vaughans have always

been very circumspect, you don't just pick up a girl at a party
and . . ."

He was holding one of her hands. Light and shadow from
the tree flickered over his face and head.

"You'll marry me, Maeve, won't you? I didn't think it would
do to ask you on the Bell System."

"But you hardly know me . . . yes . . . I think, I know, I
would love to marry you . . ." She added, on a long sighing
breath, "This can't be happening, can it? With that gray cat in
the window box staring so?"

"I know you better than I've ever known anybody. And a
girl looking as you do, right now, should not be allowed out
on the public streets. You can't go on to work shining that
way. You'd better come up to my office and have some coffee
and turn down the watts a little."

"You look a bit incendiary yourself, too, Fen. Your
eyes . . ."

The dark gray blue was silvered, radiant, under the strong
dark brows.

"Hurry, Maeve." He tightened his hand on hers and turned
her around, facing down Thirty-eighth Street again. "It's one
thing to propose to you under a tree, but to celebrate the arrangement we do need a little privacy."

Through the linenfold-carved door. Across a black and white
marble-floored reception hall, with a great swing of stairway
flying upward. Past the fascinated gimlet-eyed gaze of the
receptionist-switchboard girl — "You again, Mr. Vaughan, good
morning again, Mr. Vaughan" — up three floors in the small,
creaking iron grillwork elevator, which somebody had caused
to work again. Turn left, turn right, a sunlit office paneled in
pearwood. And into his arms, and a profound and passionate
silence.

Sitting in the rented dark green Ford parked across the street
from Fenway & Vaughan, occupied to the point of invisibility
behind a wide-open road map of New York State, Daniel Cooley
indulged his habit of murmuring, conspiratorially, aloud to
himself.

"Now, then. Desmond, nothing much new. Robert Flaherty
came through with twenty-five hundred dollars. And that girl
of yours, Maeve, talked to me on the plane as if I was a
bootboy, but what do you suppose she does on an April day,

in the street, for all the world to gape at? I thought I'd see how she spends her mornings, just an idea. . . . You'll want to know more about the fellow, won't you? . . . Happy to oblige you, but now it's time for a pint, we'll go thoroughly into the matter, later, Mr. Desmond Banbury Byrne."

FOUR

"There's a man who wants to see you, Mr. Vaughan," Mrs. Conant said, from the doorway. "I have him in my office. I don't know. I hardly think . . ."

Mrs. Conant's instincts were usually sound. She was aware that writers could be disreputable-looking persons and was not put off stride by the occasional unshaven cheek, shaky hand, or less than pristine necktie.

She added, "He says he's a friend of Miss Devlin's. Does the name Devlin mean anything to you?"

She had been having a tooth crowned during the morning and didn't know that her employer's comfortably furnished and well-ordered office had become for a time a private bower. And as he never asked her to place his personal calls for him, the name was new to her.

Fen, who had been having considerable difficulty concentrating on the manuscript in front of him, and had just had to go back and reread seventeen pages to pick up and trace a character he had mislaid, said, yes, he'd see the man.

So that, he thought, was what a sidle actually looked like, he had never seen one performed. The tall bony man came in with an apprehensive sideways movement, as though he feared an invisible hand would push the door shut in his face before he got safely inside. He closed it behind him, carefully and softly.

Fen had gotten to his feet; he stood behind his desk, waiting, studying the small dark eyes and the nighttime color of the skin, somewhere between gray and sallow. Slept-in-looking suit, crow-black; a half-smile showing bad teeth.

The voice was harsh but trying, now, to be ingratiating.

"She's a grand girl, Maeve, isn't she? I told your bodyguard out there we were friends, otherwise she wouldn't have allowed me the pleasure of making your acquaintance, I'm afraid." A street voice, with a brogue.

"Maeve?" Something about the way he said it made the man blink and move back a step.

"Well, we'll be formal, then, will we—Miss Devlin—although she was pleased enough to drink down the scotch I bought her on the plane last night, in fact we were having such a fine time of it a Boston lady ordered us to take our party to the back—"

The flickering of his eyes, taking in every detail of the office, returning again to the silent man opposite him, rather suggested that he had robbery in mind and was trying to figure out where the wall safe was.

He lowered himself into a chair and said hospitably, "Sit down, sit down, Mr. Vaughan. Grand office you have here, fine painting that, over the fireplace—your father? There's a considerable resemblance, especially about the brow."

"What," Fen asked unsmilingly, "did you want to see me about, Mr.—"

"Cooley. Daniel Cooley. Your faithful servant. Yes, I'll not waste your time." He represented, he said, an organization called the Blessed Union, whose goal was the unification of Ireland by peaceful means. "Not a finger lifted in violence, you understand, our people go out like missionaries to the savages . . ." He seemed to warm to his subject and went on at length. ". . . may take years but not a drop of blood to be shed. Street services . . . ah, the sweet balm of love and peace, the girls, God bless them, leading hymns and airs, it'd make your throat choke up to hear the innocent singing . . . of course, we need funds, the good people of your country, many of them, are happy to lend their support. A fine building, this, your name over the door, and I thought, seeing you know Miss Devlin . . ."

"You thought wrong," Fen said coldly. "If I want a worthy cause to put some money in, I don't have to go more than half a block from here to find it." He walked to the door, opened it, and stood holding the knob. "As you were able to make your way in, you know your way out."

Cooley got to his feet in a leisurely way, shrugged, grinned, and said, "You can't win if you don't play, can you, Mr. Vaughan? I get many a boot in the rear but put up with it I must, it's a cause I believe in. Good day to you."

He moved past Fen, in a strong aura of beer, and went stiff-leggedly out.

Fen was disturbed by his own reaction of resentment, dislike, and distaste. What had Cooley's purpose been, coming here? His Blessed Union sounded like a spurious and sudden invention; and he had looked neither surprised nor disappointed at his curt dismissal.

He didn't think Cooley believed in his cause, or believed in anything but Cooley's immediate welfare. Remembering the long, rogue's face, he thought the forelock-pulling amiability was assumed. There was something cold and sly and purposeful behind it.

The unreal joy of the day, the feeling of his mind and body not being here, in this office, but close to Maeve, his own discovered and claimed and lovely Maeve, clouded and chilled.

He hesitated, then dialed her number at work. He was informed that she had gone out somewhere and hadn't left a number where she could be reached—"If I've told her once I've told her a thousand times," the annoyed female voice added, "how would it be if *everybody* came and went at their pleasure, as she does?"

It would have to wait until he saw her this evening. And anyway, it was unimportant, a mosquito bite.

Another voice in his mind, which he angrily refused to credit, said, What do you really know about her? Miss Devlin, of Dublin and Manhattan.

Irish unification . . .

". . . six o'clock in the morning, are you up to your knees in Guinness?"

. . . a sort of cousin, I suppose. You shall know all about him if you like.

Daniel Cooley? With his cheap thick rumpled black crow suit and long gray teeth? Impossible. "She was pleased enough to drink down the scotch I bought her . . ."

Maeve?

"But you hardly know me . . . yes, I think, I know, I would love to marry you."

At a quarter to seven, she opened the door to him, alight.

"I thought the day would never be over, when was this morning—a month ago?"

She wore something long and soft and misty green. A scent of freesias came up to him when he took her in his arms and bent his head to her. It was she who quietly took her lips away from his. Her hands left the back of his head and dropped to her sides.

"Fen? What is it, second thoughts?" Standing very straight, she smiled at him. "Don't worry, it was a nice idea, but you're not under contract, no one's signed anything yet."

"Don't be ridiculous, Maeve." The words came out more hotly than he intended them, because he was taken aback at the accuracy with which she read—in his face, or mind, or touch—something he wanted to conceal.

He was just beginning, "It's nothing, but we might as well clear it up. There's been this man—" when the telephone rang.

Someone named Janey on the phone. "Yes, I am . . . Oh, yes, very nice, the same one who . . . All right, tell me then, of course I have a moment . . ."

Unlike her, to linger on the telephone when he was there. Staving off something? Not wanting to talk about Cooley?

He poured himself a drink, turned, and caught a glimpse of her face before she gave him only her back to study. White skin, the glowing hair loosely spilling, falling free; but she looked as if someone had just struck her a hard blow under both eyes.

Restless, uneasy for the first time in her apartment, he went to her bookshelves, stroked the silky red spine of *Alice,* and noticed a row of books in identical blue-green bindings on the shelf above. He took down the one on the left. *A Spoiled Man;*

the author, a Michael Bye. The name was only vaguely familiar to him. The publisher was British, Almsby and Orme. On the flyleaf, "Love, darling, D."

He reached for the one on the far right, the twelfth in the row, *The Goner*. "Love love love love love love love love love love love love, darling, D."

D for Daniel? He was suddenly aware of a grinding headache. Something badly wrong, his mind wasn't functioning. He had been completely clear and sure about everything this morning, and was floundering out of his depth now, or was it the other way around?

He put *A Spoiled Man* on a table for future reference and went over and gathered up Maeve, telephone and all, in his arms.

"Please stop chattering."

"I'll call you later," Maeve said. She sat down in the corner of the sofa. "Where were we? Clearing something up. There'd been this man—Desmond, was it?"

F I V E

"Who is Desmond?"

She stared at him, then gave a long sigh which he didn't understand at all.

"Cooley, his name was," he said. "Daniel Cooley, a horrible man who walks sideways and uses your name, quite intimately, and came to beg for money, from me, for some obscure and I think fake Irish cause. Something about a Blessed Union . . . but he looks as if he would be more at home with a rifle than a hymnbook. I don't know why it bothered me except he's hardly your style . . ."

She got up and went to the window and stood with her back to him. He turned her around and found her cheekbones patched crimson, her eyes flashing dark green fury.

"How dare he, how *dare* he—" out of a tight throat. "And how you could possibly, even for a minute, think—but as you obviously did, and never questioned it—I met him once, two years ago, in a pub, said, as I remember, hello to him and turned away. And was his victim, last night, on the Boston plane because people wanted to sleep and he wouldn't go away and it's hardly my style, either, to throw an unwanted drink in someone's face, even though I was tempted to—"

Her anger felt to him like a cleansing and refreshing shower, washing Cooley, and the doubts and mysteries Cooley had brought with him, down the drain.

He touched the flaming color in one cheek and said, "I've never seen you in a royal rage before."

She moved her shoulder away from his other hand. "Don't condescend, please, and find me amusing. I feel invaded, and soiled . . . fix me a drink, if you will."

"I am not being condescending and I don't find you at all amusing, but quite formidable," he said. "What I principally want is to get that look out from under your eyes."

The telephone rang again.

She said, a little desperately, "I can't . . ."

He answered it. Soft, unfamiliar, civilized voice. "We've found her party for Miss Devlin. She'll be on the line in a moment."

"Someone's been found for you, Maeve, in Ireland, I suspect, from the accent."

"Tell her to cancel it, please," Maeve said.

"Why? Who is it?"

"Brenda. I was trying to reach her and tell her I was going to be married."

He held the receiver patiently. Another voice, rounded, rich, and warm.

"Maeve? Darling, how are you?"

"No, it's Fenway Vaughan, you don't know me, I am going to marry your niece."

A short pause, and then, mildly, "Are you indeed?"

"I'll put Maeve on."

She took the receiver from his hand. "Brenda, hello, it's lovely to talk to you, how are you . . . a cocktail-hour misunderstanding, sorry to bother you."

Crisp anxious sounds; a few feet from her, he couldn't hear what was being said by her aunt.

"Yes, he did think so, and I did too," Maeve said, "but the man actually doesn't know me from Adam, we met not two weeks ago, and I think he's just conceived the idea that I have a bomb in each pocket and am planning to explode an automobile in front of an orphanage . . ."

Outraged, he took the instrument away from her. "I don't know you at all and I hope you don't find this impertinent, but she is beautiful and I love and need her and want to spend the rest of my life with her."

Three thousand miles away, Mrs. Thomas Delanoy sighed aloud. "Both of you, stop writing a play at me. Mr. Vaughan—are you sober? Are you solvent? Are you in good health? I like your voice, what I've heard of it, but you could be—no, perhaps you couldn't, she's not all that approachable. Unfortunately. I've of course wished her comfortably married long before this."

He smiled at the telephone. He liked the sound of Mrs. Thomas Delanoy.

Maeve took it back again. "I won't keep you up, it's pushing midnight, for you . . . No, of course you can't, from there, and anyway I'm supposed to be a grown woman. I won't see him for a week or two and then when the smoke clears, we'll find out if there was anything at all . . . Yes, Brenda, yes, I will, good night."

To Fen, she said in a cool, tired voice, "I was going to cook asparagus, and I thought ham, but—"

"A week. Leave out the 'or two.'. . . You're not serious?"

"Yes, I am. One accidental meaningless man, and you think, who is she, what do I know about her, I was about to offer my name, my honorable-from-1680-on name, to a woman who's really a stranger to me. A secret associate of disreputable people. Possibly mixed up with extremists, terrorists, men at home with rifles, after all she's Irish. I saw your face—"

A searing sense of her loneliness, and the vulnerability under the surface ease and independence, came through to him. Growing up, without parents, without anything warm and for granted, familiar, and safe, that could be called family. Shuttling, as she had told him, winters and summers, from her pleasant firm Aunt Kay of New York and Connecticut, dead now, to her kind rich vague Aunt Brenda in Dublin. Perhaps she felt herself something of a stranger to everybody.

Until him. Or, before him, until—who?—Desmond?

Her sudden calm briskness was somehow more disturbing than her anger. "Your poor languishing lilacs, I must put them in water."

She lifted the great fragrant armload, found a large cut-crystal bowl, filled it at the kitchen sink, and thrust the branches in without ceremony.

"And your champagne—I'll save this for whenever . . ."

Thump, into the walnut rack mounted over the drainboard.

"May we go out and eat something, quickly? There's a place just around the corner—"

"Yes, we can. Is it the kind of place where the human voice can be heard, in case we want to talk about a thing or two?"

"It's usually quiet enough—will you listen for the telephone while I change?"

Through the narrow opening in the bedroom door, she went on:

". . . in case Janey calls back. A very old friend. Her husband's just left her, which was why I rudely hung on. She hadn't known him long, before they were married, and then she found out"—a rustling sound as a garment was either pulled off or put on—"that he'd been badly in love with somebody else and turned to her for comfort. Now the other girl, whoever she is . . ."

There was a short silence, and then a desolate, "Oh God, why bore you with it, why should you care? Knock on any door."

"Maeve, for Christ's sake come out of there before I come in after you."

"I'm ready." She looked as if she had tried not quite successfully to get rid of the softness and shine. Dark blue silk pants and tunic, a dark blue trench coat, the clear bright lipstick put on by women who have no intention of being imminently kissed. Coolly intending to complete the evening one way or another, without the self-betrayal of any more gestures indicating pain.

"You seem to have formed quite an affection for that book, Fen. You can take it with you, if you like. Don't be too severe about it, you couldn't rate it any worse than he does, he says it's only his whiskey money."

He.

They walked to the small rose-lighted Italian restaurant through an evening that had turned cold and windy, with rain beginning.

"A glass of wine, please, and spaghetti," Maeve said when they were seated by a rain-running window and menus were thrust upon them.

"Two," Fen said to the exhausted-looking waiter. "Maeve, you're playing that nice Greek game called kill the messenger. I tell you something you don't want to hear and you neatly lop my head off. What's all this about?"

"It's about two people who don't really know each other and agreed in haste to marry. Under a tree. We'd been separated, the stage was all set—"

The waiter smacked down two plates of smoking spaghetti in front of them, and poured red wine with a shaky hand.

At the next table, in one of the little silences that occasionally falls on the buzz of a busy room, a woman said to the man across from her:

"Jesus, the man I hate most in the whole world. And I'm sitting having dinner with him. And I'm married to him yet. For nine lousy years."

Maeve lifted her glass and sipped her wine. She looked into Fen's clear eyes. There was no change in his expression but she felt him flinching from the gust of hate and rage.

"Do you see?" she murmured. "One should marry carefully . . ."

"Never," Fen said. "Never, never . . ."

He swallowed half his wine, looked severely at the glass, and put it down.

"This is all a little confusing, but I think now—tell me if I'm right. You thought someone named Desmond had gotten in touch with me, and you sighed—with relief, I suppose, when you found you were wrong. Someone named Michael Bye inscribes his books to you with love, and signs himself D. A pen name, Bye?"

"Yes."

"Why?" he asked, out of professional curiosity.

"I have no idea, other than that he was born secretive."

"Is D, Desmond, then, your sort of cousin, your Guinness man?"

"Yes."

"I don't want the bomb in the other pocket to blow up in my face, but in a sentence—without prying, just to get rid of the matter—who, again, is Desmond?"

"Desmond Byrne. Yes, this wine is horrible. I apologize. Brenda's cousin Genevieve married again, her husband had a grown son. We met when I was twenty-one. When I loved him and wanted him, which went on for much too long—years—he didn't want me, not to marry, I mean. . . . Then, one spring, he did. Then somebody called me up from London and said, 'You'll never guess what Desmond did last Monday.' "

"Maeve, stop. I said, in a sentence."

"He's not married any more. And now that I'm . . . free of him, he does want me, or says so anyway. And I do not want him and will not have him. It's as simple as that."

"But he doesn't accept it?"

"Whether he does or not is entirely beside the point."

"And your suburban men . . . ?"

"Perfectly real and perfectly true, all two of them. As I told you, not for me, and I couldn't help measuring them against him, and he was—is—in many ways quite marvelous."

"We might as well clear the lines completely. Cooley . . . ?"

"A creature of his," she said contemptuously, with a flare of nostril that amused him, even in his own distress. "He said, for his work—spy thrillers, sex, sadism, violence, the usual, as you'll find out when you dip in—he needed the real thing. He'd go drinking and fraternizing with touts and pimps and all the sorts of people you think about when you turn a rock over and find what's underneath . . . and then I think he got to like it, the danger, the"—she thought a moment, and brought out the word she had come to associate with Desmond—"the darkness."

"Eat your spaghetti."

"Thank you, but—" She spread butter on a small piece of bread, looked at it, and put it back on the edge of her plate. "Eat yours."

"Now I think I'm beginning to understand." He glanced again with disfavor at his wine glass, signaled the waiter, ordered two scotches, and reached over and very lightly touched her cold hand.

"You felt like this, the way I think, I hope, you feel about me—once before, about him"—he found in himself a peculiar dislike of saying the name Desmond—"and it all fell on the floor and broke."

"Yes."

"And I came in tonight and you felt as if it had fallen on the floor all over again."

"Yes. I did."

She stared fixedly at the piece of bread on the edge of the plate and then slowly and mechanically, without tasting it, ate it.

He watched the lowered lashes. "Did you hear what I was saying about you and me, to your bewildered aunt, or were you too angry to catch it?"

"I heard."

"Not fair, Maeve, look at me. . . . Have you been thinking about it at all? I mean every word of it."

She surrendered her eyes to him. There was an unguarded warmth and softness waking in them, a generously and openly declared love.

"Yes, I've been thinking about it, so much so that I'm not quite sure what I've been saying to *you*. . . . I'm sorry, but I thought I had lost you, and I couldn't bear it. . . ."

"Blowing up orphanages," he said, smiling faintly. "I see I will have to get used to Irish overstatement."

He laid bills and change on the dinner check. "Let the waiter drink the scotch, he looks as if he could use it. As I measure it, your week of separation is up and your smoke has cleared. Our smoke, that is. Come on, Maeve, darling, I'm taking you home."

SIX

Maeve woke in the night, wondering for a drifting second what she was so happy about, then lightly leaned over and kissed the strong satiny back. She felt him stir.

They murmured in a delighted rediscovery of each other. After a while, hearing a lift in her sleepy whisper, he thought she was smiling and verified it with his finger ends.

"What . . . ?"

"I don't know if I mentioned it—you're an accomplished lover, Fen Vaughan," she said.

He made his way, over eyelids and cheek in the dark, and found her mouth, and laughed a little.

"Is that a criticism, implying a licentious life, or a compliment?"

"A compliment."

"We have a saying in this country, Maeve Devlin Vaughan, it takes one to know one."

"Not necessarily. You don't have to be a connoisseur to know a good champagne when you taste it."

"That reminds me. I did put it on ice when I finished locking up your apartment."

He switched on the lamp beside the bed, walked handsomely and comfortably naked across the room, took the white toweling robe from the hook on the inside of the bathroom door and pulled it on.

He went out and came back with the beaded foil-topped bottle and two tulip glasses. She sat up, mouth corners holding a soft kind of joy, watching him pull the cork, her hair tossed and loose, against the yellow-striped pillowcase, her shoulders tenderly white.

"Happy wedding breakfast, Maeve. I suppose it is breakfast, it's four o'clock."

"And happy wedding breakfast to you. How nice, how lovely, with the rain coming down . . ."

They touched glasses. And looked at who they were and where they were, in the light, after the sweet darkness. Something moved over his eyes, like the swift shadow of a passing cloud on a sunny landscape.

"Yes," she said.

"Yes what?"

"I think I always knew what it meant, that look in the eyes, but only vaguely . . . and then Colette spelled it out for me."

"It's wonderful, what you can pick up in books," he said. "Drink your wine, love, you have half of this bottle to dispose of before you renew your marriage vows, I take this man—"

She finished her glass with gusto.

"Save the rest for the guests, Fen."

"All right, I will. You can be thinking, while I put this back on ice, exactly what day and date, preferably early next week, we will go through the formal ceremony."

Daniel Cooley found himself very tired of his perusal of the New York State road map.

"I haven't the whole day," he said impatiently, aloud. He had an appointment with the notions buyer at Altman's at 10:15.

Probably a waste of time, this vigil across the street from her brownstone, but you never knew. Kissing a woman in that way, on the back of the neck, in the public street, and she the lady, indeed—all right, I'll take your scotch, Mr. Nobody Cooley, just to save a fuss, but I won't drink a drop of it. . . .

It wasn't a waste of time.

At a little after 9:30, the plum-painted door at the top of the steep flight of steps opened and the tall figure in the dark blue pin-striped suit emerged. He ran lightly down the stairs and turned north. I hope you had an enjoyable night, Mr. Fenway Vaughan.

The Devlin woman, from what he knew of her at secondhand, didn't take men into her bed at the drop of a hat. Desmond should be interested. Very.

Fen successfully resisted the Michael Bye book until after eleven o'clock.

It had been a delightfully domestic morning at Maeve's. Using her shower, and her soap, and her towels, and her razor; reading her New York *Times*, or trying to, between watching her every motion as she efficiently cooked sweet, crisp, grease-less Irish bacon, eggs steamed in butter under a tight lid, toasted currant buns, and a pot of strong fragrant coffee. They ate at the round table in the corner of the living room, with the sun streaming in and lighting his lilacs, now lovingly arranged.

They were perfectly happy and at ease together, with only the sharp sudden stab of passion, at an unexpected meeting of glances, to disturb the peace.

"You'll call Brenda? Today?"

"You seem to feel that makes it somehow official. Yes. I will. And while we're on the subject, I won't want white, I don't want a wedding for other people, I'd like it quiet and small and simple, is that all right with you?"

"Of course."

"You haven't asked, but I'm an R.C. —ecumenical, my own style, I promise not to rattle rosary beads in your face—so it will have to be in church, if you don't mind."

"Not at all, I'm not anything in particular, I was brought up mildly Episcopalian—"

"Naturally," Maeve said with a smile. "Well, in any case, the short service—it doesn't last more than twelve minutes or so, it ought to be quite painless—"

"Painless. Marrying you . . ."

"I suppose at thirty-five you don't have to worry about any possible family objections to this unknown woman?"

"I'll probably call my father. He'll come down, he's pleasant, you'll like him."

"I knew you had a father but I don't think I even know his name."

"Charles," Fen said. "Charles by name and Charles by nature. Gray hair, well-trimmed mustache, a touch of weary elegance thrown in for good measure but he's quite hale and hearty, likes to play the Vermont farmer when he's not working on his memoirs."

Lovely, kissing her good-bye in the sunlit living room, turning to the door and swiveling around to kiss her good-bye again, and then again, soft in his arms, silent, melting.

"Go to work, Fen. Hurry."

He noticed the dark green car and the man with the wide-open road map. Déjà vu, always a strange feeling. Maeve in his arms and a green car and a map . . .

A hole opened up in his otherwise busy morning. His lunch date wasn't until one o'clock. He reached for the Michael Bye book and started, obsessively, reading.

Maeve's description had been accurate. First-person narrative. Sadism and violence, a gun on every other page, a lot of filler about chases in cars, a cruel death in an ore smelter by page eleven; the tone tough, crisp, understated.

She hadn't told him about Merlin.

Merlin turned up on page thirteen. She had a warm, white, welcoming body. She had dark green eyes and dark red hair. She was what "I," Rafe Larkin, called his "forever girl."

She had a small scar near the elbow of her right arm—he closed his eyes for a moment and tried to remember. Yes, there was a scar there.

He read on, fast, skipping, his lightning eye roving the type for the name Merlin. Larkin, an agent for something, or a counteragent, he didn't trouble to investigate the matter, took his adventures and misadventures all in stride, never raising an eyebrow; making remarkable recoveries from an attempt to kick him to death, a knifing in a London pub, a floor giving way under him in an abandoned warehouse.

Girls and beds everywhere, but he always returned to Merlin.

"They're nice bodies to visit, but you're my home, Merlin."

Page eighty-eight, Merlin's breasts and thighs and exactly how they felt in an icy mountain pool where Larkin, having escaped a pursuer, was busily making love to her under water.

"Mr. Vaughan," Miss Conant said. Silence. Heavens, he was intent, and a little peculiar, pale, and he had come in this morning looking so well, and bursting with something—happiness? Or perhaps just a particularly good night's sleep, and it was another lovely day.

"Mr. Vaughan. Fen."

He glanced up then, but she didn't think he really saw her.

"Carol Coe's come in to quarrel about her book jacket. She's had her nose fixed and she says the photograph we're using doesn't look at all like her, and as usual we're behind schedule—Mr. Weaver says will you please come down and help him put out the fire."

He called Maeve after a stormy but successful session with Carol Coe.

"Don't you get an awful chill making love in icy mountain pools, Maeve?" His tone was light and quizzical. "I would think you'd end up with the sniffles."

She sounded quiet and composed. "I've never made love in a pool, and, in case you read farther, I do not stand at the stove, naked, cooking bacon, splashing my rib cage with hot fat. I skipped a lot, but I do remember that. It's a sort of private joke of his, Fen, my sexual antics, but I never could take it seriously enough to get mad about it."

And surely, he told himself with great firmness, she wouldn't have let him have the book at all if it was a detailed journal of her physical relationship with Michael Bye, with D for Desmond.

"Are you in *all* his books? 'They're nice bodies to visit, but you're my home, Merlin.' "

"I don't know, he tells me I am . . ."

"He tells you you are what?"

". . . that I'm in all his books. . . . I have to take it on faith, they're not the kind of thing I read. He sends them to me ritually. The one you have is the first, or is it the second, I did manage to force about half of it down, but then . . ."

I do not want him and I will not have him. It's as simple as that.

"To hell with Michael Bye and all his works," he said in a strongly lifting voice. "I'll see you no later than six. Don't, please, make any dates with anybody. At all."

"Mame has a book," she said. "I have a date. I love you, Fen."

She wasn't able to get Brenda until after six, when Fen was

making drinks, managing this quite skillfully with one hand while the other arm held her.

Mrs. Locket, Brenda's cook-housekeeper, answered first.

"She's in the tub, I'll get her out. What's all this, you're going to be married, you're not going to be married, are you or aren't you?"

She was never amiable; and now her rumbling voice had a distinctly scolding, injured note. She had been a familiar, capable, and beery presence in Brenda's house since Maeve had been brought there at the age of two, when a large and unexpected green wave in the Irish Sea drowned her father and mother in their sailboat.

"Yes, I am, it turns out, Mrs. Locket." Some flickering of caution made her add, "Somewhere around Christmastime, I think . . ."

"Well, good luck to it," without enthusiasm.

"Thank you, Mrs. Locket, and may your glass always be filled."

"Here's your aunt, all soaking wet."

"What a quick week, dear," Brenda said. "I assume you've some sort of announcement for me?"

"Yes. We are. Going to be married, that is."

The sweet lilting voice came clearly through to Fen, who had not removed his enfolding arm. "Good, then, you know your own mind by now, what's he like? I hardly slept the wink over eight hours last night, consumed as I was with curiosity. . . ."

Maeve gently removed herself from Fen's embrace.

"Go somewhere and close your ears."

He crossed the room to resume his study of her books.

"Thirty-five," Maeve said. "Articulate, brainy, a sort of . . . stunning physical presence, and tall, and how can I put it, fine . . ."

"So far," Brenda said, "you could be describing Desmond Byrne." Her voice was calm and neutral.

"No, no, not at *all*." She cast a startled glance at Fen, so totally, so reassuringly different. "Mrs. Locket isn't at your elbow, by the way?"

"No, she's off to bed. Go on."

"No resemblance whatever. Kind, and quite open. Dark, fair-skinned, good everything, mouth, forehead, hands,

voice—this is impossible, Brenda, he's right here in this room,
I'm sure he can support me, he still owns part of his company,
which sounds confusing but I'll explain it all by letter . . ."

"Put him on, Maeve."

Fen took the telephone wondering if he was expected to
place a formal request for Maeve's hand. He said, "Good evening, Mrs. Delanoy, or no, it's later than that—"

"I don't like to sound parochial," Brenda Delanoy said, "and
there are probably pages of Vaughans in the Manhattan telephone directory, but—considering Maeve's overall description,
there's something vaguely familiar—are you by any chance
related to Charlie Vaughan the publisher?"

Out of a brief and astonished silence, he said, "Yes, his son,
but I never heard anyone call him Charlie."

There was a soft murmur of laughter in his ear. "It must be
almost twenty years since I've seen him, lovely man, beautiful
dancer as I remember, he was here for several months, on
business he said but it was mostly parties with his writers and
his poets—well, then, that makes it so much pleasanter, doesn't
it. I shall quite look forward to seeing him. And you, of course.
Remind Maeve to write me. When, where, all about it."

Maeve was nothing like as surprised as he was at the international coincidence; but very pleased. "Brenda," she said,
"knows everybody. Or, that is, she has a theory that there are
only one hundred and sixty-eight people in the world and they
all know each other, or are friends of friends. Just like, in a
way, my passing your building for two years and then our
meeting at a party neither of us wanted to go to."

"I think," Fen said in a slightly dazed voice, "I almost understand what you, what both of you, mean. . . ."

He kissed her for a considerable time and then said, "You
said some very nice things about me. You left out the sweat,
and the lust, and the mole on the back of my neck, and my
touching blind faith and trust in you after Cooley called, with
his Blessed Union . . . and my extreme possessiveness and
occasional horrible temper— What was that, about Christmastime?"

"Mrs. Locket—Brenda's housekeeper—prides herself as a
gossip to be relied upon. I just thought I'd pass along some
misinformation to confound her."

He accepted this as part of the Irish and giddily metaphysical
atmosphere which had temporarily taken over.

"And I gather I bear no resemblance whatever to some other man of yours, which is comforting— As far as timing goes, you have under a month, or when we leave for London you'll be traveling with me in a state of public scandal."

"Hello, darling," Mrs. Locket said. He was the only person in her world she called darling. "Hold on, I'm just making my cream sauce, I'll put it into a double boiler and it will sit there safe and well while we chat."

She had a long mournful face, a falling-away chin which misled the unwary about her powerful will, a good deal of graying red hair gathered up on curved combs any which way, and a deep voice which seemed to come up from the region of her navel. She had never been seen in her kitchen without a large crystal mug of bitter within easy reach. The tall Georgian house on Merrion Square was run by her with razor-edge efficiency.

"What's all this?" Desmond Byrne demanded. "Maeve shacked up with someone? What do you hear at your end? I got a call from a man I know, in New York—"

Mrs. Locket made an automatic shocked sound.

"Mind your language, Desmond, darling, such things are not to be thought of by decent people much less talked about." She hesitated. She hated to be the one who broke it to him. But better her, understanding him, caring, than some sudden loose tongue. "Somewhere around Christmas, she's to be married, or so she says—"

"Married," he said.

There was a long echoing silence on the line. Mrs. Locket found herself holding her breath.

"We haven't been cut off, have we?" She knew quite well they weren't; she thought she could almost hear the beating of his heart.

"Married . . ."

She wished he was here, with her, so that she could cradle his beautiful head against her breast, and stroke his hair, and comfort him. In motherliness, she told herself, fiercely.

She went on in a rush, "But Christmas is a long way off. There's many a slip. Young women today don't know their own minds. There was that man, Lafarge was it?—disgraceful, he was married, nothing ever came of *that*—"

Desmond had recovered command of his voice. It was cool

and clear. "Come on, love. I want to hear all about *this* one,
everything you know or just happened to overhear . . ."

Mrs. Locket took a deep draught of her bitter.

"His name, well, you'd know that, I suppose, is Fenway
Vaughan, and . . ."

Peter Collins, his agent, was also helpful.

"I have a good friend at Kincaird in New York—they own
Fenway and Vaughan. I'll ring you back."

Nothing much he didn't know already, from Mrs. Locket's
perusal of Maeve's letter to Brenda; except there was one new
piece of information.

A sister, Lois, living in London, married to Gaymere, yes,
the Gaymere, Edwin Gaymere, rich as God, she was ten years
younger than he was, they had been married for eight years,
no children, house in Belgravia and a place in Surrey they
almost never used—"Gaymere's of course up to his ass in
making money morning, noon, and night. . . .

"In fact, now that I think of it, I know someone who knows
her quite well," Peter Collins added. "She's supposed to be
something of a beauty."

SEVEN

"Here's Fen going to marry an Irish bog maiden," Lois Gaymere
said, reading her letter. She supposed that Maeve Devlin was
a perfectly nice acceptable girl, but it was hard to get Edwin's
attention at breakfast, and a touch of drama might help.

Trann looked up sharply from his dry cereal, which he had
been eating with a loud crunching noise. He had been breakfast-
ing with them since the first threat came in the mail; he was
seldom more than a few feet away from Edwin Gaymere.

Trann acted not only as her husband's chauffeur and valet,
but also as a confidential secretary and now as a bodyguard.

Gaymere remained absorbed in his letters, silently inserting
sections of grapefruit into his wide thin-lipped mouth. He was
a tall, heavy-shouldered man with a big bulging forehead now
all the more prominent because of the climb of the gleaming
naked skin to the center of his large balding head.

When people were informed, There's Gaymere, the financial
boy wonder, president of his own company when he was twenty-
five, now he's chairman of Greatorex, he's only thirty-nine,

they own everything, I believe they've just bought Scotland—their reaction was, What boy wonder? He looked as if he had never been young. Impossible to imagine the heavy-lidded gray eyes behind the black-rimmed glasses blinking up from under the frill of a baby's bonnet; impossible to imagine the big powerful rumpled body—he cultivated the rumpled look, as suggesting constant activity, even though his clothes were of the best—learning to dance, or bicycling, or blithely climbing a tree.

It turned out that he had, after all, heard her. "I suppose by that you mean she is of Irish nationality."

"No, American, but relatives in Ireland, she was mostly brought up there."

"Trann, the car at nine-thirty. Reservations for the two of us on British Airways to Paris as close to five as possible. The gray stripe and dinner clothes. . . . What's her name?"

"Devlin."

"Devlin, Devlin . . ." He knew of no large money interests or chimes of power associated with the name and dismissed it. "I won't of course be able to go to the wedding, but you're perfectly free to run across."

"No point, Fen's coming here on his writer-visiting trip, as he did last year, he'll have the same house in Chelsea, Alan Fort's house, we'll see them then. . . ."

"One in the bosom of your own family, sir," Trann said, and laughed his high giggly laugh, odd sound from the tall thickly muscled man with the light yellow eyes in a face of pitted red rock. "In that connection—anything unpleasant in your morning mail?"

Gaymere's next planned stop on his carefully laid-out course was the Houses of Parliament. In furtherance of this, he had written for a year a weekly column of national and political opinion, "One Man's View, Presented in the Public Interest by Edwin Gaymere, Chairman, Greatorex, Ltd." The column ran in a newspaper owned by Greatorex.

Three weeks before, he had come out with a savage attack on Catholic extremists in Northern Ireland. His life had been threatened twice since, once by telephone, once by mail, both threats of unidentified origin, the letter demanding a total retraction in "One Man's View," or else Mr. Edwin Gaymere would come to a sudden and violent end.

He had seen to it that all this was well publicized in the press and on television; he noted with objective approval his screen presence, forceful, cool, uncompromising. He called in the police and discussed the letter with them; it appeared subsequently that the writer's fingerprints were not in the files of the Criminal Records Office. He published the letter in his column, along with a transcript of the telephone call, with polite blanks where the obscenities had tumbled out of the receiver.

"Nothing this morning, no," he said to Trann. "Pack of nonsense, hysteria, in any case."

"A woman in the British Embassy in Italy got a hand blown off this morning, opening one of those letter bombs," Trann said thoughtfully.

"Any fool who can read knows by now what to look for, she's probably the sort of woman who wanders into heavy traffic too."

He rose invulnerably from the table, having consumed the last grapefruit segment and drunk his one cup of decaffeinated coffee. He went over to Lois, bent and kissed her, and gave her this morning's portion of her measured moments of his day, concentrating on her fully.

"Get a present for them, you're so good at that, always the right but unexpected thing. You look marvelous in that blue. She's probably a charming girl, Fen's a man of taste, he's had four years to look about him. How will you amuse yourself this evening, I don't want you sitting by your fire alone."

"A party, I think. A last-minute thing. It might be fun. . . ."

He had chosen her very carefully and had been given no reason to regret his choice. Beautiful in her quiet, blue-eyed, dark-haired way, long New England and Charleston bloodlines, an excellent hostess, well educated but not given to any dangerous, quirky, boil-and-bubble ideas. Serene in her world as it was, a wife who took her share of him with apparent pleasure and contentment, who was proud of him, leaned on him just enough but not too much to cause any undue pressure.

She watched him as he strode from the room. She supposed she should be frightened for him; but he seemed so untouchably strong and sure, and then Trann was with him always. She really couldn't imagine, under any circumstances, anything out of his control happening to him.

A thought from nowhere wandered into her mind. Do I love him?

How silly, the question had never presented itself before. It was probably the glorious, young May morning, lacy light and shadow pouring in, swaying, sparkling, through the blossoming rose-pink hawthorn in the walled garden at the rear of the house. Or perhaps the letter from her father, about Fen. How would he be feeling today, his marriage only a few days off?

To be in love, in May—her mind closed firmly.

Time to see to the flowers. The hyacinths on the Louis XV table in the hall had definitely had it. Tulips, perhaps, white ones . . .

"Oh, dear . . . Gaymere," Brenda said. "How on earth did a daughter of yours come to marry that computerized hobgoblin, Charlie?"

They were amiably drinking martinis in Fen's large, long, handsome living room. Fen was at the piano, playing Gershwin idly but well, with Maeve beside him on the bench. The atmosphere was tranquil.

Fen and Brenda, upon her arrival, had exchanged searching looks, and then fallen suddenly into a mutual warm natural hug.

She was an unworriedly plump woman with large fine features, delectably rosy skin, and water-clear eyes of an astonishing lilac-blue. Good nature emanated from her like a personal perfume. She wore a very beautiful suit of thin smoke-gray wool; her sumptuous pearls assumed a casual, throwaway air about her smooth throat.

Charles Vaughan studied her with affection.

"Devlin, Delanoy?" he had asked when Fen called him and told him he was going to marry and that the aunt remembered him. Then it came back clearly, a young lovely woman madly in love with her barrister husband, the big house, the parties where you met everyone, painters, poets, writers. He even remembered going up the great marble staircase to get a book from their library to confront someone about a misquotation, and finding at the top, at three o'clock in the morning, a silent leggy child.

"Do your father and mother know you're up so late?"

She had answered matter-of-factly, "I haven't either," and it took him an explanation from Brenda to catch up with that.

He lit Brenda's cigarette. "She—Lois—had had a rough love affair and was still in rags about it when she went off to London one spring. She met Gaymere, he went after her with his notorious powers of concentration, and you can fill in the rest for yourself. We didn't particularly want it—another country, and we never exactly took to him—but as you know, as far as what *you* want, after the age of twelve or thirteen, forget it."

He was Fen's height, and as remarkable to look at, with his open-air lightly-coppered skin and eyes like his son's, the color now of wet slate. "The two of you together are almost too much for me," Brenda had told him. "You give the impression of a whole roomful of handsome men."

"But Gaymere—from what I read about the man, he's asking on bended knee for a bomb or a bullet. I also gather from people who know him that he's quite above the sound and the fury, his patriotic interests in Belfast are purely a matter of personal ambition."

"What's your hope, Brenda, about Ulster? Not that I can't guess."

"Of course, I wish we were all one country, but, a tragedy, I can see no solution whatever," she said with a shadowed face. "Not in my lifetime, anyway . . ."

She reached for her glass and held it gracefully lifted. "Let us go on to merrier matters. Maeve and Fen . . . to two-thirty tomorrow at St. Thomas More. I had a nice chat with Monsignor Villiers there—a friend of a friend—and it ought to be very nice. He will marry you himself. There will be just a ripple or so of music, a little Handel never hurt anybody."

Fen smiled back at her. If there had been any last, lingering doubt at the back of his mind about the prudence of marrying a woman he had met just seven weeks ago—or about D for Desmond, and Michael Bye—Brenda Delanoy's urbane and kindly presence would have served to banish the doubt completely.

PART
TWO

ONE

The ghostly wooing began just three days after they arrived in London.

As he had done for the past several years, Fen took his writer friend's house in Chelsea. "It's pleasanter than a hotel, you can come and go as you please, it helps, for entertaining—you won't have to lift a finger, Maeve, there's a cleaning woman thrown in."

Fort went, every May, to his villa in Italy.

"In case you haven't read him, he writes travel books—very personal and colorful, *France and I, England and I, Italy and I*—he still has the rest of the world to cover, and he's up to his ears in royalties."

The annual journey was part business and part vacation. Fen would lunch with, dine with, listen to, and if necessary extend an editorial helping hand, and murmur of cheer and money, to any perplexed or doleful writer on his gilded list.

Fort would take only nominal rent. "After all, dear Fen, you published me when I'd been *spurned* by six houses. . . ."

The few stipulations were that the occupant walk his magnificent brown standard poodle, Mac; say an occasional kind word to his black and white cat, Doll; and see that Mrs. Gossamer didn't neglect the watering of his forty-seven house plants and hanging baskets.

Number 11 Polperry Mews was an attractive house, three-storied, plastered and painted gray with a coral-colored door. The white window boxes were filled with coral-pink geraniums; white petunias bloomed lustily on the high wrought-iron balcony which ran along under the bedroom windows, and from which hung floating streamers of ivy.

By mutual consent they bypassed Fort's own bedroom at the garden-overlooking back of the house—crammed with silver-framed photographs, hung all around, ceiling to floor, with stiff ballgown skirts of white satin, and startlingly decorated with mahogany racks holding at least three dozen antique guns and revolvers—in favor of the large comfortable guest bedroom looking out on the cobblestoned mews. This was done in white and blue; no eavesdropping personalities hovered in its comfortable and delightful air.

It was, Maeve agreed, very much more pleasant than a hotel. The long windows open, white silk ninon moving in the breeze, a soft scent coming in from the pale blue brick house next door, all but buried under yellow and white climbing roses.

Any-hour attacks on Fort's well-stocked larder, juicy fresh peaches he had left for them, foie gras, marvelous cheeses— "Help yourself to wine, my dears," one of his numerous notes left about the house said, "I'm sending back cases and cases, my cellar, modest as it is, wants cleaning out." His cellar was a whole wall of openwork walnut in the pantry off the kitchen, filled with bottles of the best vintage years. Fen, studying the labels, said, "Mostly too irreplaceable to drink. After cleaning up a bottle or so to oblige him—hand me two glasses, please— we'll buy our own."

There was the twenty-foot-long wall of books in the drawing room to browse through. And the garden to sip the just-opened wine in, read in, dine in: walks of white stone chips, circles and squares of brilliant soft box-edged grass, stone urns of geraniums and petunias and roses, a shell-shaped foundation on the high rear wall, its bricks invisible under a robe of ivy that stirred and rippled in the breeze like water.

Mrs. Gossamer came in every morning for two hours to tidy,

wash dishes, and attend to the plants. Maeve had tried to resist doing no housekeeping whatever, but Fen had said, "Let her do everything, Fort is as finicky as a cat, what if you broke one of his Royal Doulton dinner plates, you'd ruin us."

She was a small gray-haired woman in her fifties, fortunately taciturn, limiting herself to "Good morning, madame. Another fine day, madame."

It was nice to be called madame; Fen's. She found to her great pleasure that he was going to be a delightful man to live with. His domestic manners were gentle and fastidious. He was of an optimistic, open nature and got up each day with a freshly minted willingness and curiosity and relish in the moment. He was very close to her, mentally and physically; but he allowed her, so delicately that she was hardly aware of it, the privacy she must occasionally retreat to and rest in.

In the house of a stranger, with a man she loved but was not yet completely acquainted with, she felt very much at home.

The third night, after dinner, they took Mac for a long walk. Down Oakley Street, left into Cheyne Walk, the Thames glistening blue-silver in the bright evening light. Along Chelsea Embankment, stopping to look up at a superb house, sniff a huge white rose poking through the iron railing of a formally planted precinct, read with fascination a chalked message on a slate outside a solemn secretive brick house: "Wanted, information on any person seen entering or leaving this house between the hours of 7 and 9 on 15 March when the elderly occupant was murdered, London Metropolitan Police." Across the Vauxhall Bridge Road, and on into Pimlico. Finally, thirstily, into a large welcoming pub near St. George's Square, the Spread Eagle.

"I believe you've earned a whole pint, Maeve," Fen said. "We've done at least two miles so far."

She never forgot a single detail of it. The contented sigh as Mac sank, at her feet, under the broad table in front of the comfortable tufted black banquette. The glow of apricot-red light through the fringed silk shades, shining warmly on Fen's dark head as he stood straight and tall, his back to her, getting their pints of bitter. The William Morris-looking wallpaper, richly black, patterned in green-leaved red carnations. Smoke drifting blue against the apricot, four men intently playing cards across the room, looking like a scene from an old movie; beyond the large square opening, another room, where pop music thumped loudly and heavily, pumping like the pub's own heart, from a machine lighted eerily in ashy lavender and pink.

The record stopped just as Fen got back to the table.

He said, "Thank God for that, anyway," and then sighed as a shadowy figure leaped to feed coins to keep the loud heart beating.

They were so absorbed in each other that Maeve couldn't have named the moment when the heart stopped again and human noises emerged, a match striking at the next table, voices, laughter, a half-swallowed oath from one of the card players as a hand swept up a wrinkled pile of pound notes. A woman to the left of them calling to someone three tables down the banquette, light clear English voice, "Do you see Ruth?" Another fluting voice, "No, I don't *see* her, I phone her, I feel safer on the phone. . . ."

Mac gently and inquiringly touched noses with a Welsh corgi who had just arrived. Another pleasant human sound, someone playing a piano in the next room, not visible through the wall opening. Cole Porter, Rodgers and Hart, Lerner and Lowe.

Fen emptied his heavy cut-glass mug. "I want another one. Will you?"

She was just opening her mouth to ask for a half pint, when the song began.

Tinkling, soft, haunting. "The Young May Moon." Irish; she had no idea how old it was, or who had written it.

"Maeve. What's the matter—"

"Nothing—"

"You looked suddenly a little green, are you sure . . . ?"

"It's these pinky lights, you look an odd color, too . . . As a matter of fact, I think I'll go to the ladies' room while you get my half pint. Or the toilet, as they so flatfootedly call it."

She went around, past the bar, into the front room, and looked over at the man at the piano. Plump, dark-haired; he finished off "The Young May Moon" with a flourish of keys. She looked at every face. Strangers, all of them.

Coincidence, just a pretty and obscure song the plump man had happened to remember.

She was back in a few moments, hoping her face, now, was all right. It must be; the slight anxiety left Fen's eyes.

"Bathrooms when wanted are wonderful institutions. Here's your bitter. Cheers, my darling."

*   *   *

"Just the two of them, I think," Lois had said.

"Too personal. I dislike personal evenings."

"All right, the Clydes too. And Tom. Will that suit you?"

"Admirably."

Approaching the dinner engagement with the Gaymeres, in a taxi, through the soft blue rainy evening, Fen said, "Brace yourself. This will not be the most entertaining dinner party of your life, although Lois will do her best. He is not gay in any sense of the word; and he is not at all mere, but very conscious of his importance."

"I know about him, he was the cover story in a magazine I read at the dentist's, weeks before we met . . . he has every reason to expect a knighthood and takes indigestion pills, besides setting himself up for assassination."

"I assume you won't draw your sword and fence with him?" He asked it amiably, studying her in the hazy tiers of fawn chiffon, close beside him in the tall roomy cab, smelling delicious, one shoulder bared, the chiffon sheathing the other, her hair glistening rose and bronze and lilac when the streetlights found its shine.

"I only argue with people who think the way I do, otherwise it's a complete waste of breath," Maeve said.

"Well, as long as you're prepared . . . the main thing we have to hope for is that the soup tureen won't blow up in our faces."

When they got out of the taxi, Maeve looked thoughtfully at the ample honey-colored Belgravia house, its front nobly pilastered, its grass flawlessly green and smooth, and its roses gleaming in the rain, under tall plane trees.

"Are you sure this isn't a limited company or an embassy of some sort?"

"No, I have reason to think somebody lives here." He lifted the lion's head door knocker and let it fall full strength.

Trann opened the door.

"Lost the butler?" Fen asked. "We've all fallen on hard times. Good evening, Trann—Lois, dear—" He put his arms around his sister and kissed her heartily.

He had tried to explain to Maeve about Lois, ". . . she stopped, at twenty-four, when she married him, she's like a pretty pond frozen over. . . ."

During the introductions Maeve took her quick private reconnaissance of Lois. Her face, perfectly oval, creamy, curiously still—guarded, or just naturally calm?—her fine dark blue eyes deep-set and smokily lashed as Fen's, under a lovely high rounded brow, her mouth, different from his, the delicate corners held in secretly. A tranquil beauty, bought and paid for—cold horrid thought—Edwin Gaymere looming behind her, breathing power and money, while he said felicitous things to the two of them in his low crisp voice.

". . . and this is Edwin's brother, Tom, Maeve . . ." He looked not unlike Edwin; but nice, quiet, and perhaps too patient for a man in his middle thirties. He was, it turned out later, head of the research department at Gaymere House, in the City.

Trann stood back, leaning against the doorframe of the great candlelit mirror-flashing room opening off the entrance hall. Maeve was a little disturbed by his watchful yellow eyes, and his stance as of an animal braced to spring. She wondered if he wondered if she had a revolver in her small bronze-beaded bag.

The Clydes were cool and toothily handsome, talkative. He about grouse and pheasant, fox and badger—conversing with Mrs. Clyde, Maeve heard Fen say, "To be truthful, the only thing I believe in killing is a respectable bottle—" She about gardening: "*Do* you plan a greenhouse, at home? It's invaluable, one gets such a start on things, I've tried to persuade Lois to—but she just pops around the corner and spends fortunes on—" She gestured at an immense arrangement of lilies and roses and carnations sending perfume at them.

An unreal evening from start to finish. They had not, it emerged, lost the butler, Bellington. He and a serving maid were very much in evidence during the polite and very good dinner. A clear soup (the Sèvres tureen did not blow up), duck with oranges, a salad of water chestnuts and cucumber, a lemon meringue, fruit, cheese, the wine going from pale to rose to amber red.

Trann at the table, looking like a failed prizefighter in his dinner clothes. Edwin Gaymere talking to Fen about a publishing company in New York he thought of acquiring. Lois with an eye for everyone's comfort except for the moments when she disappeared into herself—

"Lois, come back," Fen said over his Camembert. She smiled uncertainly at him and went pink, and drew a long shaky breath.

"Just hoping the cherries won't be sour, will you test them for me, Fen?"

Into a briefly fallen silence, Maeve could be heard saying to Angela Clyde, about her morning, coming out of St. James's Park, ". . . I don't really care for the trappings and trimmings of war, but the household cavalry, going up the Mall in the sun, clanking and clopping and all glittering, the splendid seats they have, on the splendid black horses . . ."

The casual comment of a visitor to Britain, talking to someone she had just met at a dinner party.

"You don't care for the trappings and trimmings of war," Gaymere repeated coldly, bending his head to address her. "I assume that in your peaceful Irish way . . ." He had listened carefully to her enunciation, soft, and musical, exact; not placeably American. She sounded like any well-bred, well-educated Dubliner. Anglo-Irish descent, possibly, country houses and international viewpoints, but one never knew where one stood with them; there were no grounds whatever for optimism. ". . . I assume you prefer destroyed property—and wantonly disposed of men, women, and children, on both sides?"

She felt Fen, a foot away, stiffen.

"No, I do not, Mr. Gaymere."

Lois said anxiously, "Oh, Maeve, call him Edwin, for heaven's sake, he does have a first name, formidable as he sounds—"

Maeve went on, in a quiet voice, "I don't believe in the destruction of any kind of valuable property, particularly human life, for any reason whatever."

"Good." Gaymere took a sip of his wine. "Then you agree de facto that our armies are necessary. There's nothing—" he waited while Bellington refilled his glass—"like force, is there?"

"I'll take brains and wit to force, any day," Maeve said.

"Then you'll lose, any day," Gaymere said.

"Fortunately, Maeve's a graceful loser. I know, I beat her at backgammon before lunch." Fen bit into a cherry and said, "Very sweet, Lois, nothing to worry about—and one can only hope her choice is the right one, Edwin, for the history of the future, or otherwise forget the long-term prospects of your publishing house, and the rest of your holdings, they'll all be efficiently atomized."

"We now hear the man of books speaking to us of the practical world," Gaymere said. "Let us listen closely."

Maeve saw Tom Gaymere smile a little, to himself.

Fen's face was calm. "Books, since you mention them, have been written about the inexplicable vanishing of whole civilizations."

Angela Clyde, who had been trying to pay attention to her husband on the price of decent horses, abruptly joined in.

"I like a good book occasionally."

(Not a long time after the dinner at the Gaymeres', she would say, to the man from Scotland Yard, "I was only half listening, but I do recollect something along these lines—she hates the British Army, and Edwin, Mr. Gaymere you know, said she approved of the destruction of men, women, and children . . . and *he*, Fen Vaughan, was talking about everything being blown up, but I hardly imagine—he's American, and terribly attractive, and literary, thinks of nothing but books. . . .")

Fen continued blandly, "By the way, Trann, would you mind temporarily disconnecting whatever listening device I just found under the table while attempting to touch my wife's hand? I don't plan this evening to say anything for posterity. And I have no sinister designs on Edwin, however our opinions differ."

"Trann, for *God's* sake . . . !" Lois began explosively. "This is ridiculous, shall we go into the other room for coffee?"

Maeve found it reassuring, as they moved into the firelit candle-blooming room, to feel Fen's fingertips just above the small of her back, lightly propelling her, a gesture openly possessive and loving.

It was during coffee, and the sedate pouring of brandy by Bellington, that the flowers arrived.

T W O

A small incident; and out of all proportion disturbing and em-
barrassing.

Trann again answered the door and came back with a large
white box five feet long.

"Surely not a child's coffin?" Fen asked.

"No, flowers for Mrs. Vaughan," Trann said. "You'll excuse
me if I take them into another room to open the box, just in
case—"

"How *fascinating,* to be pursued about London by boxes of
flowers—unless it's something that's ticking, meant for
Edwin," Angela Clyde said, staring at Maeve. "But, then, of
course, you're on your wedding trip, Fen, what fun, did you—"

"No," Fen said. "No, I didn't."

Trann came back with the box and presented it to Maeve.
Edwin Gaymere interrupted himself in a discourse on silver
bullion. A silence fell on the room as Maeve lifted the lid.
Under the silky green paper, layer upon layer of spring flowers
delicately beaded with water and feathered with fern, daffodils,

narcissus, pink and white and yellow tulips, blue hyacinths, snowdrops. The scent of them struck her like a blow.

"Better look to it, Vaughan, two weeks married, are you?" Clyde's long leathery face was creased in a sly smile.

It obviously occurred to no one that a man had not sent the flowers.

Maeve glanced up into Fen's eyes, found the small white envelope, opened it, read the card, her heart beating uncomfortably.

"Love wherever you are, always, darling. D."

The strong spiky handwriting; she wondered if Fen could read, from above, not only at a sharp angle but backward.

Without taking time for thought, she put the box on the floor, walked over to the fire, and threw the card in it.

"Do go on, about silver, Edwin," she said. She felt suddenly very much alone, among staring strangers. Some explanation was immediately necessary about the burning of the card.

Lois said, "Bellington, if you'll just put them in water—or will they be all right in the box, they look so dewy—"

"A baroque gesture from an old acquaintance," Maeve said. "Actually I have no use for them, will you add them to your collection, Lois?"

"Yes, thank you, my bedroom is bare of its usual flowers."

There was a sudden and to Maeve unexpected sympathy, almost complicity, in her dark blue eyes, as though she was saying, I do know how you feel, isn't it awful. . . .

For the first time since she had met him, she dreaded being alone with Fen.

Talk brightly, extend the evening, listen to Aubrey Clyde, continuing on the subject of horses. . . . Desmond taking a fence, on Juno, looking appropriately like a young Apollo, the sun on his fair head, familiar Desmond, known Desmond, dug so deeply into her past. What was he trying to do to her, with people, a new family, and their guests looking on?

Yes . . . strangers. But the man who had just sat down next to her on the crewel-embroidered loveseat was her husband.

The time came all too rapidly when manners required an exit. Gaymere would no doubt have reams of paper to attend to before he slept. Fen had been composed and pleasant, talking well, as he always did when he chose to open his mouth, watching with interest Clyde's eyes dwelling increasingly on Maeve in her waves of chiffon, in her white soft grace, and

Angela Clyde's discontented mouth as she, too, watched.

"Lovely evening—" "It's been *so* pleasant—" "Maeve, you and I must meet for lunch when Fen is busy entertaining one of his writers—" "Good night, Tom, good night, Edwin, does Trann sleep outside your bedroom door?"

And then they were in the taxi.

"Maeve, you looked, you still look, a little frightened of me," Fen said in a light quiet voice. "And that's the last thing in the world I want. Forget the flowers, if that's what's bothering you."

Love, then, would have its occasional hazards too: your face and mind and emotions, trying for decent concealment, being read with close accuracy by one particular pair of eyes.

"I don't like question marks between us," she said. "They were from Desmond."

"Why? It isn't your birthday, I know. Is it some anniversary of yours I don't know about?"

"I haven't any idea. Badly misplaced affection, which I doubt, or malice, mischief—"

He was looking out the window at the rain, his head turned away from her.

"I was under the impression that he lived in or around Dublin. Does he come here?"

"Yes, often, it's his second city, he used to have a flat somewhere—"

"How would he know we were dining at my sister's?"

"Again, I have no idea, Mrs. Gossamer was nearby when Lois called yesterday, perhaps she got a call when we—or when I was out and passed the information along—"

"Either that or he's following you—us—around town. How peculiar. Unless, and I'm sure you'd say so if you had, you've been talking to him yourself."

"No, I haven't. Fen, please turn your head around to me."

He did. He looked for a long moment into her eyes and then took her hand into both of his, strong and warm and firmly enfolding.

"As I said . . . forget it. I will not have my wife in a state of distress, beaten over the head by tulips and daffodils."

She smiled uncertainly. He added, "We're almost home, and then I can comfort you."

Somewhere in the depths of the night, he woke. She woke

too as he crossed the room to open the window wider and then came back to bed.

"Sorry . . . it was hot in here. Go back to sleep. Or, as you are awake, I've been thinking—you don't know Lois, but did you notice anything about her, in particular?"

She had; but something, perhaps the memory of the fleeting sympathy in Lois's eyes, held her back.

"She's lovely, of course . . . and she seemed not to like the company of that sinister Trann, but otherwise—"

"Funny," he said. "I think of you as almost frighteningly shrewd. Well, I'm not sure her pond is still frozen over. I've had an excellent opportunity to study the subject myself, at close range—she looks to me very much like a woman in love."

Maeve was silent. The same idea had occurred to her, more than once this evening. Lois's retreats into herself, away from her dinner table to some other, delectable place; the sudden rush of color over her skin when her brother had called her back. She could imagine, from very recent experience, the rest of it, the faint sense of inner trembling when the telephone rang, the leap of the heart at the sound of a special foot-fall, the cherishing and repeating to oneself of murmured words, the conjuring up of the look in the eyes so close to yours. . . .

"You know her every expression, so perhaps— Would Edwin have noticed, do you think?"

"I don't know, I suspect about merely human matters he's not very observant. I hope so, anyway. Well, good night, love—and good luck, Lois."

She lay awake for a long time.

Why the flowers? *Why?*

Rage, or colorful pique, at her being married at all, much less six months sooner than the date he would no doubt have extracted from his friend Mrs. Locket?

What could he hope for, apart from possible unpleasantness created between two newly married people?

Was it something he was going to keep up? Inconceivable that a grown man would spend much of his valuable time on such a vain, and frivolous, pursuit.

Perhaps the gesture tonight was the beginning and the end of it.

She fell asleep to the faraway tinkle of "The Young May Moon," played by sheer coincidence in an apricot-lighted pub.

*   *   *

The flowers were not the beginning and the end of it.

The telephone rang, late the next morning, on the bedside table, while Fen was knotting his tie in front of the oval pier glass.

Maeve sat in the chair by the window, watching him with pleasure. She enjoyed his dressing process.

"I always wondered how long it took to make everything go together so well, and how you always look so pristine . . . but you don't take half a second to decide which shirt with what suit, and what tie, you just sort of reach—"

He had been telling her about the writer he was taking to lunch.

"—have you read her? A lesbian, but amused, detached, which I've found is rare in that quarter, at least on paper—writes about her affairs so wittily that in a way you're reminded of Darcy and Elizabeth having at each other—she's probably calling now to say she'll be late, she's late for everything."

He went to the bedside table. A deep male voice, rich, resonant, leisurely. "I would like to speak to Maeve Devlin, please."

Fen stared at the phone. Rudely and abruptly, for him, he said, "There is no Maeve Devlin," and replaced the receiver with a sound just short of a crash.

She got up from her chair. He went back to the pier glass and finished knotting his tie. Dark gray and white, broad bold stripes, against the narrower gray and white stripes of his shirt. He put on the coat of his suit, a dark pitch-brown. He looked marvelous. Except for his face. It didn't have its usual open-browed, collected look.

"Have I just died?" she asked a little timidly, not being able at the moment to think of anything else to say. Later, of course, the commonsense words presented themselves, "What can I do about it, it's only harassment, not to be taken seriously. . . ."

He folded a white linen handkerchief and put it in his breast pocket.

"Your name is Maeve Vaughan now. Remember? What the *hell* is this, was that—could you hear his voice, from there?"

"Not exactly to identify . . . from here." The truth; but she thought it was probably Desmond.

"Of course, you may know other people, here in London, do you?"

"A few . . . yes."

"—who might," he said in an unconvinced voice, "not know you'd been married but who might have gotten your address from, as Brenda would say, a friend of a friend—"

"Possibly." She found herself wishing that Brenda had not gone on from New York to an extended visit to friends in San Francisco and Palm Springs. It would be nice to have someone to talk to, someone who knew about him. Someone with whom she could be free and open, and a little frightened, about all this nonsense.

"Brenda, what on earth would *you* do, under the circumstances?"

From the top of a brass-fitted campaign chest lacquered deep sea blue, he took change, a cigarette case, keys, and billfold and pocketed them.

"I think we've about had this misplaced playfulness, Maeve—or malice or mischief as you call it. I'd like to have a few words with Byrne. Maybe, if you have time while I'm out, you'll do a little telephoning, people who might know where to reach him. As you, apparently, don't."

Apparently.

But, a calm sensible suggestion. Yes, she would do that. She went with him to the door.

"If in any case you should need me for anything, I'll be at Rule's." He bent and kissed her lightly.

It was their first cool parting.

THREE

She went immediately to work with the four volumes of the London telephone directory. First, Almsby and Orme, Michael Bye's publishers. There had been, she was not surprised to find, no listing for Desmond Byrne or Michael Bye. He had still a third name he had written two books under, but she couldn't for the moment remember what it was. Sean something? No, but close.

She found a courteous, helpful woman at Almsby and Orme who laughed and said, "He's quite the man of mystery, isn't he? We have no address for him, we deal with his agent, I'm told he's rather a ravishing man—Bye, not the agent, although Peter, Peter Collins, is perfectly presentable. Here's his telephone number, and address if you'd like it."

A girl's voice, swallowing a yawn, at Peter Collins's office. Mr. Collins was out to lunch, which was apt to take quite a long time, could he call Mrs. Vaughan back? No, sorry, she herself could not supply information on any of Mr. Collins's clients without his authorization.

Next, Luke Graine, whom she had met through Desmond long ago. He owned a gallery in Knightsbridge. "I'm glad *you're* not out to lunch, Luke, everybody else is."

"Are you kidding? The way things are going, I'm lucky to have my pint of lager and bite of cheese in my office, and wait for the jangle of the bell—and how are you, love, and what can I do for you?"

When she told him, he said, "If I were you, I'd stay away from him. I don't like the occasional things I've been hearing about him. He's got his fingers in something called the Holy State, or Devine Union, I suspect he invented it himself, he's hauling in money, I've been told, mostly from the States. Gullible souls who think they're helping the cause in Ulster. And I don't care for the people he associates with, including, someone else told me, a man involved in an armed robbery in Cork—"

"I don't want to see him, I just want his telephone number, if he has one, in London."

"Sorry, I haven't a clue and don't know who could give it to you. Come and see me anyway. I have an unusually," he sighed, "full stock of highly desirable pictures."

Which concluded her short list of possibilities. She ate a peach and a piece of Brie for her lunch. The house seemed very empty. It was the first time she had been alone in it since they arrived. Doll, arching softly around a doorframe, black and white, looking in any position like a Japanese print, somehow emphasized the deep silence. Mac was asleep by her chair.

Was Fen, between sips of his martini or sherry or whatever he was drinking with his lesbian, wondering if she had slipped out somewhere to meet Desmond? Or if she had opened the coral-painted front door to his demanding presence? If he hadn't started thinking this way, suspecting, conjecturing, how soon would he begin?

Damn you, Desmond. For a short time, it had been so lovely, so secure. She tried to listen to Brenda's faraway imagined words. Cope, dear, *cope* . . . don't let other people manipulate and manage your life for you, and anyway you're not the first married woman to be admired by other men, take it in stride. . . .

Restless, she was nailed to the silent house, she couldn't leave until Peter Collins called back. He did, shortly before three.

"Sorry, I have no present address for him, he was at Dolphin Square last week, he could be in Dublin—if you know him, you know how it is with him, itchy heels. No doubt I'll hear within a week or so, I have a check for him, call me back today week. Is it important?"

She had hesitated about giving him her name; he would probably tell Desmond a Mrs. Vaughan had called, looking for him. But go through any door to get this thing over with.

"If you do hear from him before you get a mailing address, ask him to call me at this number, please." Pray God Fen would not be home if and when he did call. No, don't start thinking that way. No secrets, no whispers behind closed doors. Not with Fen. Ever. Damn you, damn you, Desmond.

She took Mac on a brief walk and then thankfully fled the house, to the Tate Gallery. Rain was starting and the wind had turned raw and cold. She paid her respects to the Turners at the Tate, as she always did before beginning her wanderings. Walking about, looking, musing, she found herself thinking that perhaps he would emerge from the stairway in the corner, leading up from the restaurant. Or surprise her from behind as she studied a Barbara Hepworth sculpture.

She must get rid of the feeling that he was everywhere, watching her every move. And Fen's. He couldn't be in two places at once, though. ". . . the people he associates with, a man involved in armed robbery in Cork . . ." Yes, Desmond had his friends to help him keep an eye on the Vaughans. If he hadn't abandoned the project.

The rain was heavy when she went down the stairway past the shining dripping Renoir nude washerwoman; the Thames, so close, had half-concealed itself through the windblown veils. No cabs in front of the gallery; she went around the corner to the bus stop on Atterbury Street and saw the tall retreating red rear of the bus half a block away. How long would it be before the next one came? Ten minutes, twenty?

Fen might now be at home, looking at his watch, waiting for her. She had left a note telling him where she was going. Of course, he would take it on trust. Of course . . .

She started walking, fast. She was soon very cold and wet, as she had forgotten to bring any boots along in her luggage. Rain whipped in under the umbrella, soaked her face and bare head.

She finally found an empty taxi, far up the Vauxhall Bridge

Road, and got into it panting; she had been half-running.

"Eleven Polperry Mews, and I'm in rather a hurry, please—"

The front door opened wide before she could get her key into the lock, reminding her of that first dinner with him, when he had been faster than the proprietor.

He put his arms around her and looked anxiously at her blued, chilled face and streaming wet hair, plastered in strands over her forehead, arabesquing her cheeks.

"God, you look awful, darling, somewhere between Undine and a drowned rat, and you're shivering . . . you didn't—*he* didn't . . . ?"

"No, nobody, only the weather of the United Kingdom, it took me ages to get a cab back and I was worried that you'd be worried—"

"I was. I didn't at all like my farewell to you this morning. I kept wanting to dash away from the lunch table and come home and restate it, properly—which I can now do."

After a while, he said, "You're still blue. Will you have a hot bath, or tea, or whiskey, or will I warm you?"

"You, Fen."

He had lighted a fire in the blue and white bedroom.

"Against my return," Maeve said, sniffing the fragrance of apple logs.

"Not against, *for,*" Fen said.

"I keep mixing up my two vocabularies. By the way, I did do some telephoning, no immediate luck, but—"

"Later."

How could she let herself have taken the morning's small annoyance so seriously, blown it up into a near nightmare; when everything was so beautifully all right again.

" . . . the only thing I can do now is wait for Peter Collins to call." She had omitted Luke Graine's gossip. It was only hearsay, she saw no reason to help destroy, verbally, Desmond's character; and besides, she didn't particularly like the picture of herself against a background of possible felons.

"Slippery bastard, isn't he," Fen said mildly.

They were having dinner at a candlelit table at a small, exquisite, and wildly expensive Italian restaurant in Soho.

He ate a breadstick flavored with Parmesan and thyme. His eyes were unclouded and intent.

"What does he look like, your passion-crazed man? In case

I spot someone obviously tailing us down a street—or if he comes pounding at the front door for you."

"Oh, tall, your height, perhaps an inch more, reddish fair hair, blue eyes, regular features, skin ruddy-tan, he's outdoors quite a lot—"

"Apart from the height, you could be talking about thousands of inhabitants of the British Isles." The waiter appeared. He ordered, and returned to Desmond.

"Come on, Maeve, I've heard you describe people, you're much more succinct than that. Don't be inhibited. I've had my tantrum for today."

"Tantrum . . . ?"

"I all but called you a liar to your face and I kissed you good-bye as if you were my great-aunt, for which I am very sorry."

This, somehow, made it harder to go on. She touched his hand on the tablecloth with one finger. She said slowly, unwillingly:

"He's . . . frightfully handsome. Golden, spectacular. People turn and stare, as they sometimes do at you . . . there's something catlike about him, large, though, not the domestic kind . . . and I don't know why I say catlike but I do . . . he has amazing blue eyes, like hyacinths, you seem to see them shining like beacons, half a block away. And in summer, a great many freckles, which look particularly out of place on a Roman nose. Fond of clothes, spends a lot of money on them, and is well turned out always."

"Well . . ." he said on a long exhalation, as though he had been holding his breath. "He sounds"—not looking at her but watching the waiter pour wine—"like one of Elissa Field's heroes. Except for the freckles, she'd never allow those, or perhaps she just hasn't thought of them. . . . I did ask for it, didn't I? I think I'd know him if I saw him."

He was, she hoped and believed, deeply asleep when the footsteps went by, and the soft whistling rose on the night air.

"The Young May Moon" . . .

Over the sudden pounding of her heart, she listened to the crisp long-striding lilt of the footsteps, the faint ring of metaled heels. She had waited with longing to hear the sound, so many, many times.

Someone was with him, a heavier footfall.

A phrase from the song floated intrusively through her mind: ". . . and the best of all ways to lengthen our days/Is to steal a few hours from the night, my dear. . . ."

A pause, before 11 Polperry Mews, and then the feet went leisurely on. Tense, sweating, she lay listening, seeing in her mind's eye night-wandering, whistling Desmond and his companion, a man from the sound of it, going down the mews.

Past the pale blue house with its roses, around the curve where houses painted pink and pale green, cream and lemon and tangerine, looked charmingly into each other's faces. The great willow weeping over the lemon-colored house and swaying out over the narrow street would be blowing and whispering in the darkness.

Had he—wild, night thought—left something on the doorstep when he paused? Something ridiculous, to enrage Fen, or something . . . dangerous?

The whistling faded into the night. A slight movement from Fen. She raised herself on one elbow. She had better go down to the door and see.

Only one sound to be heard now, a series of descending notes from some delightful singer, thrush, or dove, or nightingale, she wasn't very good at birds.

". . . he could be in Dublin, you know how it is with him, itchy heels . . ."

He wasn't.

He had just passed by, serenading her.

There was a sudden rushing rustle of sheets as Fen sat upright. "That song," his fully awake voice said. "I was half-asleep, I thought I'd dreamed it, the whistling, and then—" A hand, firm on her far shoulder, turning her to him. "I could feel you holding your breath, waiting, as if you were afraid something was going to strike you. Wasn't that the same song, on the piano, at the pub, when you looked so strange?"

"Yes . . ."

"What's the name of it?"

" 'The Young May Moon.' "

"Has it something to do with him? With you and him?"

"Yes, long ago, but then it could be anyone, whistling, playing a piano, I think McCormack sang it, there's a record, it stays in your mind once you hear it. . . ."

"Where were you going, just now? Out to follow him down the mews?"

Another voice of his she hadn't heard before. A long, bad silence.

Then gently, "No, the feet stopped in front of the house, I was just going to see if something had been left there, on the maddest off-chance."

"I'll go."

She followed him to the top of the stairs, waited while he unbolted the door, saw him, against faint illumination, bend down. Oh, God, don't let it be something that will explode, take a hand, ruin a face, what nonsense, what hysterical nonsense, this is a silly game of his, not malign, evil. . . .

He bolted the door again and switched on the hall light.

"Champagne," he said wearily. "Still ice-cold. Dom Perignon. There's a note tied to the neck. 'To us, forever, love darling, D.' He writes an interesting hand. . . . I'll put it in the refrigerator for you to drink, when it takes your fancy."

"You told me you'd had your tantrum for today," she said, looking down the stairway at him.

"I have, except that now it's tomorrow, and he'll have shot a good part of my night's sleep to hell."

He went into the kitchen and came back. She came down the stairs to him, slowly, wrapped in pale green silk, her hair tossed and soft from the pillow.

As he stood, rigid, she reached up her arms and joined her hands at the back of his neck and pulled his head down and kissed him.

"I don't know what else you need to know," she said. "About you, and me."

The bird sang again, heart-piercing sound filling the little hall.

"Do you know what that is? I don't—"

"Yes. A nightingale."

"Fen . . . ?"

She leaned against him, graceful and soft, looking up at him, everything of herself in her eyes and only for him: naked, defenseless.

He said, "Nobody's ever, really, said my name before."

The cork popped. "We'll split it, thank you, D, the fact of the matter is that you want her and I happen to have her and this is good champagne."

He lifted the bottle and poured.

"I have made a family decision, Maeve," he said, touching his glass to hers. "For at least twenty-four hours, I don't care if he lays a path of rose petals for you from here to Buckingham Palace. You can tread it, and I will keep my temper and simply look the other way."

FOUR

At close to three o'clock in the morning, the dusty black Volkswagen went down Queen Victoria Street at an unremarkable speed, not fast, not slow. It pulled in for a few minutes to the curb, at the Underground station simply marked BANK. The driver took a bottle of lager from his raincoat pocket, uncapped it, and drank thirstily. To his left, beyond, was the illumined and pillared might of the Bank of England.

He finished the bottle, started the car, and turned right, down King William Street, a gently descending hill. He passed without knowing or caring about it Wren's church of St. Stephen's Walbrook. Bells somewhere near struck three, the deepthroated ringing emphasizing the eerie silence of this angled empty jungle of stone and brick and concrete and steel.

He turned left into Cannon Street, left again into Gracechurch Street, and driving slowly, now, looked for the lane he wanted. Past Bullshead Passage, turn right, turn left, into Cutney Court.

Gaymere House rose fourteen stories high from behind its semicircle of private drive. An unlikely and thriving garden of roses and cypresses wreathed its bronze-doored entrance. The driver pulled the car past the entrance doors, which were lit by a low floodlight in the rose garden, to the farthest portion of the semicircle before it rejoined the cobblestones of Cutney Court. It was almost completely dark here. He waited. Silence. He was all ready for any question, from a policeman, from a night watchman, belligerently approaching. "I'm looking for a chum, he's on night duty somewhere around here, am I right for Brasenose Alley?"

No one approached. He got out of the car, and at a speedy but controlled pace—not hurrying, just purposeful—turned into Cornhill Street, stopped at a telephone booth he had previously selected, and fingered coins.

At Gaymere House, the sleepy male switchboard operator put down his copy of *Penthouse* magazine. He listened with a dropping jaw to the soft polite Irish voice, suggesting that if there was anyone in the building it would be a good idea to leave immediately, a bomb would go off in ten minutes.

Hands shaking, he put himself through to the night watchman. The building was quickly emptied of its perhaps half a dozen occupants.

The only person injured when the car bomb exploded in thunder and blue and orange was a clerk who had been dallying in his superior's office with his superior's secretary. He was now on his way home to Fulham, heading for the Bank station on the Underground. His amorous adventure cost him an arm.

Maeve was cooking breakfast while Fen sat considering which he would do, continue watching her, with the sun in her hair, or go down the mews and buy *The Times* from the newsagent's just around the corner.

He flicked on the radio. BBC news *and* Maeve, no further decision necessary, for the moment. Race results, cricket, and then a return to the major story, "A car bomb exploded outside Gaymere House in the City about three-twenty this morning. A warning telephone call had been received ten minutes earlier and the building was evacuated. Explosives police estimate at two hundred pounds tore down the heavy bronze doors and smashed every window at the front of the offices. Edwin Gaymere, the financier, was safely at home at the time. He has been under threat, purportedly by the I.R.A., although this has been denied. The warning call, according to the switchboard operator, was made by a man with an Irish accent. The only injury sustained was the loss of an arm by . . ."

There was a sudden smell of scorching eggs. Maeve turned the electric burner off and snatched the pan to one side.

"It's like hepatitis, or car accidents, or a house on fire," Fen said. "They happen all the time, but not to you, or anybody close to you. . . . After you've fed us, one way or the other, I'd better go and see how Lois is."

Lois looked pale but composed. She was in her own sitting room, arranging white and purple lilacs in a tall Wedgwood jasper jar.

"Good morning, Fen, how nice of you to rally round first thing. I don't suppose anyone was actually meant to be killed, do you, how awful about that poor clerk, apparently hopelessly overworked, from nine o'clock in the morning until three-thirty the next morning, *really*—"

Fen instinctively grasped his right arm with his left hand.

"Yes, horrible. Where's Edwin? Picking his way across the pavement through shards of glass, business as usual?"

"No, he was off to Johannesburg, with Trann, at eight this morning. Do they have any Irish extremists down there? I hardly think so."

She studied her lilacs, readjusted the arrangement, dipped her short straight nose into a white plume.

"Was he rattled at all?"

"Not rattled, angry about the destruction, on the surface, but actually I think in a way he's pleased, the BBC news, and there were television cameras at Heathrow when he got on his plane, and there'll be the newspapers . . . and it all makes him seem that much more intrepid, he's refused police protection again, the ratepayers' money, you know . . ."

She sounded objective, as though she was talking about a public figure, and not her husband of eight years. Fen went over to her and said, "In these letters and calls—there's never been any kind of threat against you, has there?"

"No, why should there be?"

"While we're on the subject, look at me for a minute, forget those damned lilacs, they'll keep. . . ."

The pink swept her face again, under his close gaze. She lowered her lashes protectively, but not before he saw the uneasy radiance in her eyes. Her hand, returning obsessively to her lilacs, trembled a little.

Fen said, "If you're in any kind of situation—any kind of trouble—will you for God's sake remember I'm in the same city with you?"

"Trouble . . . ?" She seemed for a moment not to grasp what he was saying. Gaymere's being in imminent danger of his life was a fact that might not really exist at all in her private world, in which he thought something more immediate and important to her loomed.

"Oh." She cleared her face deliberately and smiled at him. "Oh, you mean if there is some sort of threat, directed at me—of course I'd come running to you—"

"Do. And not only about that. If anything else erupts in your face—it's none of my business, but I hope . . . is Trann ever able to take any time from his lord and master to follow you about and see what you're up to?"

"No, not a moment of his day." She faced him squarely, both arms at her sides, but an invisible hand came out and thrust him away. They had always been comfortably close, and fond of each other; now he saw that this was a territory he was not to be allowed to set foot on. The secrecy puzzled him. Surely, with him, she'd feel safe? "And I have no idea," she said, "what you can possibly mean."

He was suddenly impatient with ambiguities. "I seem to be surrounded by women with shadowy lovers in the wings."

"Surrounded?"

"Yes, Maeve, too." It was a relief to talk about it, casually, a little irritably; to put it in its proper place. "Someone, well, you saw, sending her flowers, leaving champagne for her on the doorstep to be taken in with the morning milk, whistling *their* song to her, under our bedroom windows—"

"Oh, Fen. How boring, for you."

"Not exactly boring. We'll meet, sooner or later, and have a short discussion about the matter." He was standing against the long sunny window, facing her; tall, dark in the dazzle of green May light behind him, formidable.

"I'm a bit ambivalent about it all. I don't know that I'm fitted to take any strong moral stand, and I'm glad to see you show there's something you're very happy about, when you're taken by surprise—but on the other hand, in the role of the cuckolded husband, Edwin, or whatever his name might be, Fen, sometime, maybe—"

He immediately wished he hadn't said it or allowed himself to think it.

"Oh, Fen, she's very bright, and able, and I think strong—but the way she so obviously *melts* to you—"

"To get back to your position—Edwin has cut down whole corporations who got in his way, whole countries, as far as I know. If he found you dallying, wandering astray, you'd have no more chance than a field poppy in the path of a tractor."

"Don't worry. Nothing is going to happen to me." She sounded strong and confident. She was away again, close and safe with somebody else, who would see to it that no harm could possibly touch her. Then, hearing the cool distant sound of her own voice, she smiled affectionately at him. "I do like you in that jersey suit, Fen. And your shirt, it matches my lilacs, almost. And as a matter of fact, that tie, too."

"Thank you." He smiled back at her and touched her shoulder protectively. "Anything particularly wrong with my socks and shoes? . . . I don't need buttering up, I'm on your side. I'll be off, then, I'm glad to"—he gave her a final crisp and knowing glance over his shoulder—"see you taking things so well in stride. Come and visit Maeve and me if at any time, with Edwin away, you feel lonesome."

His meeting with his own wife's shadowy lover came sooner than he expected it.

FIVE

"Good afternoon, Mrs. Conant, is it? . . . I gather you do take such marvelous care of him—we've chatted transatlantically but never met before, have we—I'm just back from Florence, and was on my way to Harrod's, and couldn't pass the house without stopping, I thought I might find him in. Where is my beautiful Fen?"

Maeve regarded the dark slender tall woman, black rain-sparkled cape still swinging after her sudden entrance. She knew from photographs on the backs of book jackets who it was. Elissa Field, a sort of publishing landmark all by herself, one of Fenway & Vaughan's most prodigious moneymakers. She wrote immense five-hundred-page chronicles about a British family with branches in Scotland, England, France, and Italy, the Cotterings; she had set them in motion in the early seventeenth century and they were now thriving in the Victorian age.

Her books combined gusts of well-bred sex with wars and disasters, the costumes and manners of upper-middle-class life,

love affairs, and suave tragedy. There was enough wit and
solid information in her pages that one did not have to apologize,
being caught reading her; enough downright juice and comfortable warm family ambience to pull the nonreader to her as to
a magnet.

"Good afternoon," Maeve said. "Mrs. Field, is it?"

Fen had never said whether she was married or not; it seemed
an impossibility that she wasn't. Violet eyes, mysterious; high
elegant cheekbones, a small fine imperious nose, white skin,
shining black hair worn in a chignon at the back of the long
white neck. A dancer's body, strong, sinuous, a drawling soft
voice.

"Yes, then you do remember my voice—"

"I'm Maeve Vaughan," Maeve said. "Do come in to the fire."

Elissa Field stared. Not at all politely, but an appalled look,
a sudden abandonment of the notion of this other woman as
Fen's secretary, a stocktaking from head to foot. Maeve had,
still about her, the first, rich shine of her love and glowed with
it in the low-lit hall of Alan Fort's house.

"But you couldn't, I mean, how could I possibly not hear—"

"We were married a few weeks ago. In New York. Very
quietly. I don't suppose it made whatever newspaper you read,
in Florence."

"Good God," Elissa said. "A *Mrs*. Vaughan." She looked
as if she had received a severe blow indeed. "Surely you're
not an old friend of his? Surely I would have known about you?"

"No. We met quite a short time ago."

"Well. You must give me a little while to take it in—do you
expect him? Fen? I don't want to—"

"Yes, let me have your cape, he ought to be along soon,
he's having a late lunch with somebody named Dunning."

"Oh, darling Robert, yes, he'll be raising hell with Fen about
how they don't advertise enough, and drinking too much brandy
and Fen will probably have to escort him home in a cab . . .
are you sure I'm not interrupting your day?"

"No, I was about to have tea, if you'll join me."

"I'd like to, very much, as a matter of fact somehow I was
so sure I'd find Fen in that I arranged with someone to pick
me up here . . . hello, Mac, and Doll, dear, how are you,
come to greet your Elissa—the walks I used to take that dog
on, when Fen was tied up, we're old friends, aren't we, Mac?"

She whipped off her cape, showing a lithe black dress with

a strand of pearls looped low on her hips and falling to the hem. Real ones, Maeve thought.

Elissa preceded her, possessively, into the drawing room. Hanging baskets in the french windows at the far end, overlooking the garden, made a lacy, floating pattern of green against the darker gray green of the rainy afternoon. The colors of the room were soft and ghostly: apricot, ashy lavender, watery jades and blues.

In Elissa's eyes was a fond renewal of close acquaintance with this room. She sank into a velvet sofa. "So nice for you to have the house of such a comfort-loving man. Dear Alan. I think I'll have a glass of his own special sherry, if I may, you'll understand I've had something of a shock—while you have your tea and crumpets, or whatever." She smiled at Maeve. "He keeps it in that walnut cabinet affair."

Mac—disloyal animal, Maeve thought, poodles love everybody—went over and sank at Elissa's feet. Doll curled to the caress of her hand.

Following Elissa's directions, instructions, she gave her her sherry—"No, not that bottle, the one behind it, I could find it in the dark—" on a soft breath of laughter. "After Fen and I . . ." She left the sentence unfinished, floating in the air.

"Zaragosa Something on the label."

Going to the kitchen, where her tea had been brewing too long and would probably take the top of her head off, Maeve tried to decide if she always talked this way. If not, a message of a very explicit sort was being delivered to her, about Elissa and Elissa's friend and editor, Fenway Vaughan.

She brought back her tea, sat down, and took a doubtful sip. Must be calm, pleasant, hospitable; this was business, in a way, Fenway & Vaughan business.

"No crumpets? But of course, your lovely figure—Fen laughs at the way I eat, I'm a positive glutton, but so far, fortunately—"

From what seemed a long way back, "I enjoy your appetite, among other things. For a blue ghost, you consume an impressive amount of food."

She wondered what other qualities she and Elissa shared that Fen enjoyed.

They talked, with a surface amiability, about Elissa's stay in Florence, where she had been filling herself in on the background for Eva Cottering's fatal dalliance with a young nobleman after she had fled to him from her husband and children in the house in St. James's Place. Elissa seemed to take it for granted that Maeve had read all her books and knew her characters; Maeve had read none of them but kept this to herself.

"So nice, in a way, that one can work, really work, yet be in heavenly Florence, and find time for all sorts of delicious other things too. . . ." She glanced at her watch. "Speaking of delicious other things, where is Fen? Robert should be safely tucked up by now. You say you spend part of your year in Ireland, tell me about Dublin. The last time I was there the poor sweet city looked so tatty, and the smell of the fabled Liffey, God help us . . ."

Maeve told her about poor sweet Dublin. She had put aside her undrinkable tea and poured a small glass of Alan Fort's special sherry.

". . . and your aunt's house is, where, Merrion Square? Nice once, but they're tearing it all to pieces, one hears, those lovely Georgian houses—"

The doorbell rang. Elissa got up and swept past Maeve. "Do let me get it, it's probably—"

Maeve had gotten up, bracing herself for another stranger. She put her glass on the mantelpiece and stood close to the fire, warming herself. The light from the fire caught her soft floating hair, sent ripples down the length of her body, gracefully at home in a loose creamy silk tunic over pants.

Mac had faithfully followed Elissa out of the room.

She listened to the greetings.

Impossible.

The sound of the man's voice in the hall, under Elissa's high flutings.

". . . he's not here yet, Michael, come along, we're drinking sherry . . ."

Maeve stood absolutely still.

Following Elissa, her pearl rope swaying creamily from her hips, Desmond Byrne came into the room.

Just inside the door, he paused, for a moment. Elissa was saying something, but Maeve had no idea what it was.

This is no accidental meeting, she thought. He's managed it, somehow.

Desmond strode the ivory and sapphire Chinese rug to her. He took her in his arms, crushingly hard, and bent his head and put his mouth to hers, and started a long and inescapable kiss.

It was just a few stunned seconds before she began her furious struggling.

During several of these seconds, hung, long, forever, in time, Fen put his key in the lock of the front door, crossed the hall, and stood looking at the passionate embracing of the two figures standing on the hearthrug.

Time halted itself for him too. It had always been, it always would be, the brassy golden head bent over Maeve's fire-shining dark red, not two bodies but one, glistening cream and superb ruddy Harris tweed, welded and inseparable.

A disinterested observer might have noted that there was something odd about the embrace, something not quite right. Her arms were not about him, clasping his back, but were pinioned hard by his against her sides, as though she had been taken wholly by surprise.

For a terrible flickering moment, he was inside the other man, he was the other man, feeling the firm familiar tenderness of Maeve's breasts against him, her long thighs, the beating of her heart, powerfully knowing her body and letting her know his. Breathing her breath and smelling her perfume, heated now, something between narcissus and sandalwood—

Starting to move out of a stilled zone of ice and silence, he saw without putting it into context the wild jerking of her hands at her sides, one leg thrust behind her as she arched her back; heard the half-stifled cry as her mouth was taken again.

In a rage that he had forgotten was possible to the civilized, he crossed the Chinese rug in four steps.

There was a start of unaware flesh and bone under his grasp, a peat smell of rain-wet Harris tweed in his face, as he took the shoulder and tore the man loose from his wife's body.

Desmond swung around with an instant, animal response, looked, said, "You're the bloody bastard who took away my girl—" and quick as he was, was caught by a savage and accurate fist on the edge of his jaw.

He went down like a tree falling.

Elissa had been making noises, talking, all the time; sounds to which only she gave heed.

"Maeve—may I?—Maeve Vaughan, this is Michael Bye, perhaps you've heard of him, a writer—" On Maeve's being seized in her escort's arms, "Good heavens, I didn't know you'd met, and certainly didn't know that you— Come, is this some sort of joke? Although I must say it doesn't look like it—I think she wants to be let go, Michael. . . . Fen, thank God, the whole world's mad, I never knew Michael was to say the least a dear family friend, oh *God*," shrieking, as Desmond went crashing down, "this is all too absolutely *much*."

The three of them stood looking down at Desmond. The only sound was a hiss of released sparks and a mild crackle from the fire. Waves of gold played on Desmond's hair and face and his blinking blue, beacon gaze.

Very slowly, he raised himself on one elbow. "Well," he said, "and I thought adventure was dead. Here I arrive to pick up a friend for a drink and I greet another old friend, in a quiet mews in Chelsea, and the upshot is a near broken jaw"—he felt it thoughtfully—"on a Persian hearthrug. No thanks to you, Vaughan, that my head's not flaming away on the logs or broken on the hearth or the fire irons."

Fen only half heard him. He was appalled, himself, at having come so near to the possibility of killing a man, however inadvertently; he was shaken by the blaze of passion, or the semblance of it, on one or both sides, which his hand had interrupted; and with his sense of estrangement from the blue-faced woman he had married. Standing so still, arms at her sides, looking at the man on the rug.

"I suggest you get up and get the hell out of here," he said in a tired, winded voice.

"Can you, darling?" Elissa asked. "Are you all right? I must say you sound all right."

Desmond seemed to be disposed to make himself comfortable on his hearthrug.

"Talk about having the floor," he said. ". . . on what subject shall I address you? Elissa, you might look a bit less as if you were enjoying every minute of this. After all, I've been victimized."

He should have looked ridiculous, and didn't. He looked, propped on his elbow, relaxed and unhurt, strong and sure of himself.

"Maeve, love, the least you can do is get me a glass of whiskey, I'm somewhat in a state of physical shock. And a cigarette while you're about it, there's a good girl—mine are in my raincoat pocket in the car. Come, Vaughan, don't look at me like that, you can't very well hit a man when he's down."

Fen stood assessing him. "What chapter is this we're on, Bye, or Byrne, or whoever you happen to be at the moment?"

Yes, very well turned out, even at their feet, nothing rumpled or roiled about. Handsomely cut suit, cream challis shirt, chestnut wool tie, gleaming gentleman's boots, narrow and impeccable. He raised one lazy knee and dropped a long, lean hand over it.

Maeve broke her silence.

"For God's sake, rise from your ashes, you've had your scene, or both of them." Her tone, intimate in its soft fury, reminded Fen that they had been close, in and out of love, for nine years; and he had only had her for a few months. He felt very cold.

He reached down to pull Desmond forcibly to his feet and Desmond helped, with a rising rolling catlike motion, throwing him slightly off balance.

"I know where I'm not wanted, not when himself is at home, anyway. . . . Come along, Elissa, before my host calls the police, the publicity wouldn't hurt me but it's not quite the thing for your more peace-loving public. . . ."

Outrageously, he went over to Maeve and bent and kissed her hair.

"Until the next time, then, my darling," he said.

He told her, in chanting guttural Gaelic, that he hoped her husband measured up to him, in every way; and that he would like to think of her as reasonably happy and taken care of in the meantime, until—

"*Michael!*" Elissa cried, not looking at him but at Fen's face.

"Before you take yourself off," Fen said icily, "I'd like a telephone number and address where I can reach you if you continue in your career as a public nuisance."

"No doubt you would. Right now I'm on the wing. I'll let Maeve know, one way or another, where she can find me when I do have a roof over my head. Hurry, Elissa, I'm thirsty and there's no comfort of that sort to be found here."

"No fixed address," Maeve said, with the same soft fierceness; Fen turned and looked at her. "Lovely way to live, that. Next thing, making mailbags for Her Majesty, I suppose."

They went, he with a final body-raking glance at Maeve. Elissa called back from the hall, "Oh, dinner, still, Fen? I'll be at home in an hour, will you call me . . . ?"

A ringing silence, upon the click of the closing door.

SIX

They began by speaking very quietly to each other, perhaps in an attempt at recovery, in sound level at least, from the raw gusts that had swept the room.

"You haven't had a proper drink, if that thimbleful on the mantel is yours. I'll make us both one, I think I need it, having just stepped out of the ring."

"Elissa," Maeve said pensively, almost to herself. ". . . she didn't know we were married, she was outraged, as if someone had pinched some valuable personal property of hers."

She thought then that she was talking only to fill the silence but later decided her motives were questionable.

She was aware of a plain and, just for a moment, simple relief that he, too, had some emotional trailings catching up with him, deliberately exposed to unshadowed daylight by Elissa.

"Are you quite sure you wouldn't have married him if he'd asked you, even a few months ago?" Calm tinkle of ice cubes against crystal. "Are you sure marrying me wasn't a knee aimed at his groin?"

Quiet voice. Terrible words.

She had no idea how long it was before she answered him, her face unnaturally still.

"Quite sure, and he did ask me, last Christmas Eve . . . very nicely, in fact, among the candles and holly, 'O Holy Night,' not this kind of caveman scene at all. In Brenda's drawing room, children outside, singing carols, Brenda dousing them with coins and handing out ginger cakes and oranges."

She accepted the glass from his hand. "She's still quite possessive, the way she looks at you. 'Where,' she asked, 'is my beautiful Fen?' "

"About Elissa, she and I—it couldn't matter less."

"Not to you, now, perhaps. And in a way it's only fair, I've asked for it without knowing I did. You had Desmond thrust in your face, I have Elissa. Wanting Alan Fort's own special sherry, Zaragosa . . ."

She took a small sip of her drink, not looking at him, but at Elissa's face, the eyes tender, the mouth warmly remembering.

"She said she could find it in the dark, the bottle. She didn't specify *what* dark, but there was a rustling of the bed sheets in her voice. . . ."

Her own voice stopped. This is my love. This is my husband. What is happening here, to us?

He drained his drink. Maybe words, however harshly flung, might help erase the picture, still squarely in the forefront of his mind, of her, in those claiming arms. Nine years—

"Did you assume, Maeve, that I was living under vows of chastity against, as you say, the day I would finally meet you?"

"This is how, to go back to our old forgotten days, you must sound at a business meeting, articulate, in control, when you're up against an adversary. But," Maeve said, "watch out for civilized Fen Vaughan."

Three feet away from her, he was pale, and remote.

He had never before seen her eyes on him, asking, Who is this man?

" . . . as for setting yourself up in a monk's cell, no. I hadn't seen you that way at all."

"I'd hope not. The warm white welcoming body, 'You're my home, Maeve.' "

"The name was Merlin. And I believe that in your work you're familiar with the term 'fiction.' "

"Do you mean to say you've never slept with him?"

"Of course I don't mean to say that. What would you—editing something or other—think of a woman madly in love with a man for years who would content herself with a hand at the films or a knee under the tablecloth? You might be shocked, in reverse, that it was only perhaps three or four times . . . because I used to have something, in that situation, amusingly called pride."

Keep your face contained and outwardly peaceful. Don't let it crumple, weeping. Where are we going, Fen? Your voice. Your face, formal, examining.

Her legs were suddenly trembling and she wanted to sit down but wouldn't let herself.

"Well, we'll mutually concede that they're both attractive-looking people that we're mixed up with. Elissa—"

"Speaking of how people look . . ." He moved a foot closer to her and studied her. She seemed to him, in a way, sullied. Marked with Desmond. Literally. ". . . your lip is bleeding."

"Sorry, damaged goods. But as you haven't got around to kissing me hello yet, it won't rub off on you. In a moment, I'll go and wash away Desmond, and then . . ."

She tried for a casual taste of her drink that turned into a gulp, and found herself infuriatingly choking and coughing. He waited, motionless, watching her, until she recovered. Tears ran down her face.

He had not understood Desmond's parting words but he had gotten somehow, through a smile, a gesture, the gist; he was being sexually affronted.

"What was he saying to you, in Gaelic? How much he missed you in his bed?"

"Not quite. . . . We are running merrily along on our separate tracks, aren't we, side by side? That was a fine heroic gesture, but you struck him for *you*, didn't you, and not for me. Not that I don't thank you for it. He insulted both of us, though, I thought."

Fen said, "I'm not entirely convinced a woman was ever insulted by a kiss."

"You're not? Unfortunately, there's no way you can test it yourself, see how it feels, clamped so you can't move, at least move any part of you that's screaming to get away—"

"You're colorful, Maeve."

"But, you see . . . whatever he's planning . . . is working."

In spite of her distress at talking to him like this, over a cold white barrier of snow, her mind was racing and twisting, searching.

Desmond wasn't socially crude, and to her, at least, very seldom physically cruel. He had been putting on a display for some reason, or for someone—

Elissa?

He couldn't possibly have known that Fen would arrive while she was in his arms.

"What do you mean, working?"

She touched a finger to her hurt and bleeding lip. "I can talk better after I attend to this. . . ."

She went up to the bathroom and scrubbed her face, hard and punishingly, blotted blood until it stopped, put on fresh makeup. Stay here in the blue and white quiet, don't go down and face the accusing stranger. . . .

He was standing, staring out of the window at the rain. He looked as much alone, bereft, as she felt.

To his back she said, "Mischief is one of the words I used about this postmarital courtship of Desmond's. But you see, it is working. Have you been listening to what we've been saying to each other?"

He half-turned; she went on, sounding out of breath, "Perhaps I'd better leave you for a while, go to a hotel, or somewhere, that way he can't get at you through me, hurt you—"

This time, she left out the hurt to herself. She went over to him and saw the dark sadness on his face, hovering about the fine eyes and mouth.

"Fen, oh Fen, don't look that way—"

"Yes," he said. "I've been listening to what we've been saying to each other. Or, more particularly, what I've been saying to you. Looked at in another light, you have been attacked by him, your blood drawn, your arms will be black and blue and probably green too where he—and I finished it off with a heavy kick to the head. All your men are delightfully mannerly, Maeve. Both of them, that is."

"There's only one of them."

"Unfortunately," he said, "you can't throw the past out with the grapefruit rinds and the coffee grounds. But this happens to be now, not then. In a way I wish he'd stayed a comfortable specter . . . I'm sorry about quoting him at you, but to see him in the flesh . . ."

He moved swiftly to her.

After a time in his arms, his face buried at the side of her throat, his lips moving gently over her skin, he said, "Don't let me hear any more, ever, of your going away and leaving me. Drink some more of your drink, darling, you still look as if you may be going to cry. This time, if you choke on it, I'll pat your back for you."

"You must, I suppose, dine with Elissa?"

"Yes, unless it will rip another terrible hole in something. She's off to Scotland for a couple of days and there are things that have to be settled, about the new book, or at least she says there are, apparently she is not able to put down another word without my advice and counsel."

To the handkerchief in his breast pocket she murmured, "Is there a Mr. Field?"

"No, they were divorced years ago."

"Well, we'll drop her, shall we, until you have to go to her?" She added thoughtfully, "I'd hate, myself, to be limited to having you only in your editorial capacity."

Alone in the silent rain-wrapped house, she tried to read but kept coming back to Desmond and the scene before the fire.

Fen, she knew, loathed physical combat and had done what he did out of instinctive rage; but Desmond enjoyed it and was good at it. Ordinarily, he would have been on his feet in a second or so, fighting back—she could see with horror Alan Fort's ornaments flying, crashing, the *famille verte* vases on the mantelpiece, the ginger-jar lamp on the table by the hearth, the table itself, fragile faded mahogany, brass-galleried, inlaid with painted porcelain lilies of the valley and forget-me-nots.

Had it been mere panache, a display of prone magnificence to three pairs of eyes, an amused withholding of obvious power? Playing a scene with relish, perhaps for Elissa, perhaps for Fen.

Because there was almost nothing that he could do that would surprise her.

Fen saying, "What chapter is this we're on?"

Was he playing, not an isolated scene, but a role? Not Desmond Byrne, but the "I" of Michael Bye?

A man to whom nothing is impossible, who cleaves his way

through any and all dangers and obstacles, to get his man, or his woman, or his immediate object in any given book. Larkin, in his pursuit of his love, snatched from him by marriage—and no doubt in pursuit, she added wryly to herself, of the very comfortable fortune she would inherit from Brenda, which had probably always been a part of his plan—Larkin would brook no permanent interference from the man who had had the impudence to take over his girl.

A scene from one of his books flashed through her mind, a push from behind, down the fearsome gleaming double cliff face of the escalators in the Piccadilly Circus Underground station, a toppling doomed body. Fen—

She felt as if her ribs would crack with tension; she found that she had been holding her breath.

Or a sudden unseen hand between the shoulder blades as a red bus came plunging along, around a curve in Knightsbridge, an unknowing man standing on a traffic island, waiting for the light to change—

Stop, think, push back the panic. Larkin would hardly expect the suddenly widowed woman to dry her tears and bury her husband and turn to him with love. He would be her first choice for her husband's killer.

But still, a role. The flowers, the music, the kiss, which he couldn't have known Fen would witness. A plot he had invented. After all, it was his daily work, he lived with it, planning dark deeds and bizarre crimes, in which Larkin, always, emerged triumphant, by fair means or foul.

She hadn't got it right yet, not remotely; but she and Fen had something important and central to do with the plot.

Too bad she had skipped so lightly and carelessly through his books, except for the first one.

On impulse, she went over to examine Alan Fort's two six-foot shelves of paperbacks in the long wall of books. There were, she found, five Michael Byes. In one of them there might be a story or scheme she could recognize; there might even be a cue he had expected her to pick up. On the other hand, this might be a whole new, living book he was writing, about the three of them. And about someone, something, else.

She settled down with the paperbacks, skimming, scanning; she was a fast reader and raced through the pages.

Rafe Larkin steals a girl from her parents, holds them up, with her consent, for fifty thousand pounds, spends it with her while in pursuit of a Cyprian double agent and his mistress, escapes death by fire, poisoned cornflakes, and a fall into an Alpine ravine—no, not that one. He came back, on the last two pages, as always, to Merlin.

In the second, nothing to go on either; set in Africa, Larkin pursued by a pride of lions, finding Russians setting tribes against each other, something to do with an abandoned gold mine. She remembered that Desmond had spent a fascinated four months in Africa and wrote a book to pay himself back for it.

A passage in the third book riveted her.

Merlin having an affair with another man. The description chillingly accurate: ". . . he had a poet's face, the eyes mild, rainy-gray, under soft brown hair that had a way of falling loosely over his high bony forehead. Tall, a little bent, studious, peering amiably through large glasses, rimmed in black. . . . I found that, like many Irishmen, he had a poor head for drink. Thank God that's not a problem of mine. We had a couple, and then a couple more, and then a couple more. He said, 'That's enough, I think . . . I have a long drive before me,' and I said, 'Come, won't you drink to Merlin?' I gave the bartender one of my repertoire of winks. He gave Brennan a triple and Brennan said, 'Oh, to Merlin, yes, of course,' and downed it in one gulp. Poor lad, his last drink on earth, the fine fellow's car went off the road near Howth, hit a tree; a bad stretch there, I know every foot of it. But after all I was just being hospitable, you might say, any lover of Merlin's is entitled to my closest attentions."

In order to make the killing in absentia acceptable to his readers, he had cast the man with the poet's face as a British agent about to defect to Russia.

John Lafarge, with whom she had had a brief and sad love affair more than three years ago—he was separated from his wife, but she would not divorce him, and they were both Roman Catholics—had died in a welter of smashed metal against a great mulberry tree on the Howth Road.

There had been a heavy fog that night, rolling in from the Irish Sea. No mention had been made, in any account of his death, of intoxication. But then, a scent of whiskey about a man would hardly qualify, in Ireland, as a news item. And autopsies are not performed on men crushed in automobiles.

SEVEN

Desmond, encountering her in O'Connell Street a month later, had given her a blue look of appalled but possessive pity, and said, "I'm just back from New York, I just heard—poor devil, to think we had a drink that very night, I remember we drank to you. . . ."

Even then, she had wondered. Not a clear-cut question in her mind, or any kind of statement; just a faint frightful shadow of a thought. He had told her weeks before, laughingly, that, all right, she could have Lafarge for a little while, if it amused her—

She had still been going, when she was in New York, to Dr. Knorst, in her long struggle—first the Desmond years, then another man who might and might not marry her—*why, Dr. Knorst?*

His earnest, anxious face when she talked about John Lafarge, his gentle Austrian-accented voice, "Let us examine this fantasy of yours, about men killing and dying for you, Maeve. . . ."

Shortly after that she decided that she had had enough of Dr. Knorst, or he of her. Go it alone, then. She was healthy, happy in her work, and there were other men, sooner or later there would be one she wouldn't have fantasies about. One she wouldn't think of as killing or dying for her.

And finally, marvelously, when she had more or less decided to be single, and free, and content, Fenway Vaughan.

Eyes tired and burning, mind bombarded and hardly able to concentrate, she went quickly through the other two books, and found nothing that could give her a direction about what he was up to now.

She told herself firmly that as with many a writer John Lafarge's death had only been grist to a hungry mill; Desmond had merely twisted it into fiction to suit his plot.

But—keep thinking. Don't take the obvious, the tempting course, and say, Oh, God, it's all too much for me.

His voice, murmuring into her throat, came back to her. They had been standing, lovingly locked in each other's arms, just there, on the creamy medallion on the pale sapphire rug. ". . . unless it will rip another terrible hole in something." *Another*. Was the rip that bad, for Fen, that big, in the fabric of their marriage?

Did he forgive her Desmond, each time, because he loved her and couldn't help himself; but had he lost some basic and irreplaceable faith, trust in her? Poor torn, wandering Maeve, two men—"I will simply look the other way."

Sensing some sort of distress in the air, Mac came and laid his head on her knee and looked up at her with his beautiful soft dark gold glance.

She would have to find him, talk to him, have it out. Enraging that he had been here, so very much here, and had walked out the door, deliberately vanishing, no place to reach him. Perhaps Elissa would know; somewhere in the course of the evening Fen would ask her about it, surely. Unless he wanted, again, to look, very hard, the other way. Not to see or even think about his wife with her bleeding lip and developing bruises, standing amid her grapefruit rinds and coffee grounds.

When he came home, at a little before midnight, he found the eight-by-ten-inch poster, or scroll, thumbtacked to the coral front door.

"I am a member of the Irish Union," its headline said, large and bold. "I believe in the unification of Ireland," it went on, "but only by peaceful means." In an apparent attempt to liven up the cold type, there was a line drawing of a rifle with a red X across it. "Not by guns and bombs, but by love and understanding, promulgated with the help of God through the selflessly working members of the Blessed Union. To this cause, I have contributed"—there was a blank for the sum, which had been filled in in pencil—"£100. Irish Unification and Blessed Union forever."

He took it off the door, folded it, and put it in his pocket. Maeve was in bed, awake, with the light on, an open book beside her. She kept her arms under the covers. He went over and lifted one arm out and stroked the purpling flesh.

"I really spent the evening here, with you, I hope Elissa didn't spot my absence. Did you know someone left some nonsense for you on the front door? Or for both of us, rather. I thought Cooley had made all this up on the spur of the moment, but the thing must after all exist."

Maeve read it, rubbed her eyes, and said very softly, almost to herself, "Dear Christ."

"He wasn't here, annoying you—Cooley?"

"No. And do you believe that, Fen?" She fingered the stiff paper.

"Of course not . . . but why? I mean what's the point?"

Cooley. A creature, she had said, of Desmond's.

"Who knows? Plain everyday spite, perhaps—if it was Cooley, passing by—the man loathes me, which I take as a compliment. He'd have hoped that a resident or so of the mews would have spotted it and start looking at me with suspicion, talking about me. You're respectably American, you're all right, but I don't completely look and sound the part. And what will that woman in Alan Fort's house do next—throw a grenade out of the window, or practice sharpshooting in the garden? Something like that."

He started to toss the scroll into the fireplace but she said, "Save it. It's one of the things I'll want to talk to Desmond about."

He stood in the center of the room, his back to her.

"You're going to pursue the connection?"

"Yes. I must. And try to end whatever this is, once and for all. Do get yourself to bed, Fen, you look awfully tired." In any other circumstances, she would have wanted to hear about his evening; now any question, however casual, would seem awkward, prying—suspicious.

"You make that sound like a very one-sided proposition."

"Well, I didn't know if you were still—"

"I don't know how your sentence was going to end, but I'll pick it up from there." He came over and kissed her. "I am, still, and always, Maeve."

No sounds later presented themselves to her anxious wakeful ears. No ringing footsteps, no softly rising whistle. Only the rain, and the late-playing nightingale.

She wasn't entirely sure whether his delicate and tender and then passionate lovemaking was saying to her, I love you, I want you; or whether it was addressed, male to male, triumphant, to Desmond.

EIGHT

She was still not quite used to the pleasure of waking up and finding the face, or the back of the glossy dark head, so near; of seeing the eyes open, gray or blue depending on the light. Open, coming back from the far mysteries of sleep, and kindle as they rested on her face.

"There's a woman in my bed," he would say in mock wonder. "What shall I do with her? Kiss her, for one thing . . ."

This morning, she watched his eyelashes with a gaze still tired and sandy from last night's intensive reading and from having waked early, tense, worried—should she tell him? Shouldn't she? She had to.

Death's little brother, sleep. Oh, wake up, Fen, please. . . .

The lashes lifted. Blue eyes, today, dark, clear. He reached over and put a light, inquiring fingertip under one of her eyes. "What's wrong? Couldn't you sleep?"

"I woke early. There's something I ought to tell you, that you won't like hearing, Fen."

"Well, if it's kept you awake, we might as well get on with

98

it. But not on a totally empty stomach."

She was sitting, in her robe, in one of the two blue and white linen-covered chairs by the long windows when he came back fifteen minutes later with cups of steaming coffee.

"I'm as ready as I'll ever be, Maeve. What is it?"

Her voice was very steady. She kept her eyes on his.

"After Desmond—after that was under control—I had a rather bad short love affair with a man named John Lafarge, married, separated but not entirely, wholeheartedly, from his wife."

Nothing happened to his face but she felt him wince.

Defensive in spite of herself, she asked, "Did you expect an unmarked, intact ice maiden at the age of twenty-nine?"

"No, of course not, thank God you're anything but—and I assume that this is not just being told for my entertainment, another chapter in the life and loves of Maeve Vaughan." He drank coffee and waited.

"He died. A car crash. A heavy fog, there were two or three other accidents that night on the same road, another one fatal too. I went through Desmond's Michael Byes last night, trying to find out what he might be up to, with me, with us. There's a man exactly like John, Desmond's protagonist got him drunk and sent him off in his car. *Death at a Distance,* he might have called it, but he didn't. Then, not long afterward, Desmond met me in the street and tendered his sympathies and said that, just the night before John died, they'd had drinks together."

Her voice stopped. The room was very quiet. A long white ninon curtain swayed against her hair in the breeze. The rain had stopped during the night, and sun shone brilliantly on the white gros-point rug patterned with blue and purple irises.

"It's probably the writer's way of using anything at hand," she said. "I think so, I hope so, but I had to tell you."

"Are you really telling me"—he stared at her—"that you think there's a chance in a hundred that he might take it into his head to do something to me, in the way of a chance fatality?"

"When you put it into words, it sounds mad. But I thought it would be completely wrong of me to keep from you even the remotest possibility that he—"

"And what are you suggesting I, we, do? Run away home and hide from your bloodthirsty lover?"

"No." She had been through all this, in the early, wakeful hours. "He has no ties, he can go everywhere, there's no place he wouldn't be able to follow us. I want you to be careful, that's all, watch over yourself. And the other thing is, I want you not looking the way you are now, at me, when I go hunting for him. As I told you I must, last night. There are things about him that he doesn't know I know—I'm sure I can handle him. But don't, please, darling, accuse me of sly rendezvous, secret kisses, and that kind of thing."

"Are *you* quite safe in threatening him with whatever you know?"

"Yes. I think so." It was hard to say this, because it truthfully implied an unbreakable kind of bond between them.

"I'm sorry, Fen. I'm sorry about all of it." She sighed wearily, and bent over and touched his hand and said in a faraway voice, her throat constricted, "But you . . . walked up to your fate and chose it, didn't you?"

After a long pause, he said, "Yes, I did. And I won't have you in that state of woe." He got up and reached for her hand and pulled her up to him. His arms around her were warm, bringing her back to safety, reassurance, a sane sunny morning in a London mews.

"I will indeed keep my eyes open. And see that he doesn't land on the step behind me on an empty midmorning escalator on the Underground, for instance"—how strange that they could read each other's minds, she thought—"or pour colorless crystals into my drink in the unlikely chance that we happened to be side by side at a bar. No, I'm not laughing, Maeve—" He kissed her forehead gently. "I felt a streak of the rogue, that self-contained sprawl on the hearthrug, you're right about the cat, nondomestic, ready to spring. But I am quite good at defending myself when it's necessary."

The morning shed its vaguely nightmare edge. A shower for him, a bath for her, melon and broiled ham in the sunny kitchen, Alan Fort's stereo system soaking the air with Vivaldi, Mac to walk, Mrs. Gossamer, "Good day, madame—sir. A fine day for a change, madame, perhaps we've said good-bye to the rain for a bit."

Fen had to go to Cambridge to see a don who was also a novelist of distinction. "I'd take you along, Maeve, but it will be bread and cheese, and bitter and port, and then the river, miles of it, walking, while he tells me about his divided feelings about returning to his wife, we have the same conversation every year—"

"The same wife?" Maeve asked with interest.

"Now that you mention it, I'm not sure, all he ever calls her is 'she.' "

It was a day on which, as it went on, she would wish that he was not in Cambridge, but at home.

She was getting ready to go out, walk across Waterloo Bridge and go to the Hayward Gallery when Mrs. Gossamer answered the telephone before she did and, covering the receiver with a discreet hand, said, "A Mr. Byrne, madame, are you at home?"

Yes, she was, to Mr. Byrne.

"Desmond, I want to talk to you, and face to face, not this way—"

"Later, love," Desmond said. "Right now I have some rather pressing considerations for you, in case the police come knocking at your door. Is Vaughan there, by the way?"

"No. . . . And why would they do that?"

"You haven't seen Gaymere's 'One Man's View' this week? An all-out attack on the Blessed Union. He claims, the lying bastard, that it's a cover for guns and ammunition, not a peaceful organization at all. There may be people the police will now rush to get onto who think I have a sort of connection with the Union. . . ."

A sort of connection . . . he had told her once, after a good many Guinnesses, interspersed with Irish whiskey, that he had invented it, and that his disinterested attempts to come to the aid of his mother country might make him, in spite of himself, mildly rich.

"Why would they come to me? This is England, we're not known by all and sundry to know each other."

"It will be all no doubt in this evening's or tomorrow morning's newspapers, the latest aren't-the-Irish-awful story. That bloody fool Cooley had one pint too many and told me he'd tacked a Blessed Union pledge to your door, he thought it was a great joke. Some of your neighbors in the mews might have noticed it . . . and in any case the police occasionally are very good at finding out who knows whom. See Police Constable Gunning in *The Goner*. The point to be made to them, by you, is that we've known each other for years and you know of absolutely no involvement of mine with this group."

She was silent. Would it be, now, lies to the police? How far was she to allow herself to be dragged, with him, into his shadows? Edwin Gaymere, whether Fen liked him or not, was in a way family, his sister's husband.

Very softly, Desmond said, "Do you remember another fine day in May? When your horse bolted and was seriously debating taking the two of you off the edge of the cliff into the sea?"

She would, of course, never forget it. His dazzling bravery, racing after her, then off his own horse, fighting, struggling, with a wildly terrified animal, a scant four or five yards from disaster for the three of them. He had won the fight, but just barely.

"Yes, Desmond, I do."

"Well then . . . ?"

"All right. How soon can we meet, tomorrow, the next day? I must see you, I won't have flowers, I won't have champagne, I will not have you attempting to woo me up to the doors of the divorce court, or whatever mad purpose you have in mind. We are going to talk this out and then stop it cold—"

But what was she saying all right to? She might, for a little while, lie for Desmond, but Fen wouldn't, shouldn't. What if the police came while he was here? She removed her mind from the possibility. Just get along from moment to moment, now.

"First and foremost, I have my own pelt to preserve," Desmond said. "It's somewhat uppermost in my mind, you'll understand. If you stick to your sweet silence, I will get in touch with you and we will discuss these other matters, such as my romantic attentions to you. Now I must run, love."

The line was empty.

She resumed what should have been a normal morning, troubled about Desmond and about the role of potential liar being forced upon her. "No, Officer—Sergeant, Inspector, Chief Inspector?—as far as I know Desmond Byrne is not in any way associated with the organization in question." "Are you prepared to swear to that, Mrs. Vaughan?"

She noticed, going down the mews, that Cooley had left another mark of his passage. A cheaply printed Blessed Union poster, with blanks left for the dates and places of meetings, to be filled in as here, in pencil. He had glued it to a brick wall, where white roses nodded over it. Someone had torn off the bottom half.

"Blessed Union rally, 27 May, Marble Arch. Irish unification through peaceful means. If you believe—" The rest ripped away. Today was May 27. She decided the Hayward Gallery would keep, took a tall rocking red bus down the King's Road to Hyde Park Corner, and walked up Park Lane, enjoying the architectural splendors and oddities and extravagances in the brilliant sunlight, to Marble Arch.

She bypassed a speech about the abolishment of taxation and another one about the liberation of homosexuals and found the Irish Union rally, a small straggling group. Anything less war-like could hardly be imagined. There were two pale underfed-looking girls in tan uniforms, with Irish Union emblems in green stitched to their sleeves. One of them delivered the by now familiar message: ". . . spread of peace and light and love and understanding . . . we need your prayers . . . we need your help, your money . . ." A young policeman stood near, hands clasped behind his back, listening blandly.

"Bloody murderers!" a woman screamed. "Blowing up in-nocent people! Up the Orange!" Another woman, evidently an Irish Union advocate, turned and poured out abuse of her. The Irish Union girl who was not the speaker handed around paper cups of weak tea—"Don't drink it," someone called, "it's probably poisoned, deadly oil of shamrocks in it." A strong, male brogue; Maeve smiled to herself. Such tea as was wanted having been dispensed, the second girl started to play "The Mountains of Mourne" on a harmonica and a few voices sang unevenly to it.

A small man, also in a tan uniform, was taking pictures with a battered camera. Maeve supposed they were for documentary evidence that, yes, there was an Irish Union, see them at work, now, at Marble Arch, spreading peace and love.

It couldn't cost much to run a setup like this and pocket the rest of the funds—if, that is, they didn't actually go into guns; but again guns could be sold for a profit. The underfed girls might well be volunteers, getting nothing but their meals and uniforms and transportation; they had the devoted gray-skinned look of unpaid help.

"The Mountains of Mourne" ended, and the harmonica girl passed around a little shallow straw basket. Her takings looked to be about half a pound at most. Maeve refrained from adding a coin or bill for the enrichment of Desmond and Cooley and whoever else was in this scheme with them.

The sad thing, she thought, was that the poor girls probably believed what they were preaching, every word of it.

Too nice a day to go home, to a house without Fen, and think about Desmond and his flight. Would he go to ground in Ireland, or sink deep into London? His Rafe Larkin, she remembered from last night's Michael Bye seminar, was a great man for disguises, had turned himself into a filthy coal carrier, a beer-soaked idler with a liver-colored birthmark disfiguring his face, a gray-bearded stooped man feeling for the pavement with the white cane of the near blind. "People," he wrote, "tend to look away from the dirty, or pained, or maimed, or unpleasantly marked man. . . ."

She drank a half pint of bitter and ate a sandwich of Cheddar cheese sprinkled with mustard cress, on the delicate firmly textured light brown bread of British pubs, in the Rose and Crown just off Piccadilly, walked up Knightsbridge and into the Kensington Road, and deliberately straying, finding alluring crescents and lanes and angling charming streets, walked all the way back to Polperry Mews.

It was then after four o'clock. She found that a worried Tom Gaymere had been waiting for her for an hour, sitting in his modest Ford Anglia in front of the house.

"I'm terribly sorry, Tom, I've been gallivanting, it's such a lovely day—and before we settle down inside, I must take Mac out—"

"That's all right, Maeve, I had hoped to find Fen here, is he not at home today?"

"No, in Cambridge, fix yourself a drink, I'll be back in three minutes, hello, Doll, come on, Mac."

When she got back, he said, leaning against the grand piano, "I really shouldn't be bothering you about this, you couldn't—but I thought that Fen—"

His long face looked pale. His brother's face but the portrait done with a gentler, kinder brush. Nice good-humored mouth, quiet eyes behind the tortoise-framed normal-sized glasses, not Gaymere's great black-rimmed discs.

"You didn't get your drink. I think you need it. I'll join you, to urge you on with it."

He sighed. "Well, then, scotch for you, is it? You'll want ice, where's the kitchen, I'll get it for you—"

"No ice. Go ahead, Tom."

"It's probably nothing, just a change of plan I can't right now account for—but Edwin's gone."

NINE

"Gone? Gone where?"

He couldn't possibly mean that Edwin Gaymere was dead.
A heart attack . . . ?

"I don't know," Tom Gaymere said. "He was planning a
long weekend in Surrey. He was to drive down this morning
with Trann. Two Japanese businessmen were to lunch there
with him, something about Far Eastern Airlines, he's thinking
of buying them. He didn't turn up for lunch. His housekeeper's
been on the phone to me, she doesn't at all know what to do
with these men, apparently they're quite upset about being
stood up. Edwin"—he took a deep gulp of his drink—"Edwin
is never late to anything. Ever. Edwin never mixes up his
appointments. *Ever.*"

"Wouldn't Lois know? I gather she didn't go down with
them, with Trann and Edwin?"

"No, she was to go down tomorrow, she had a dressmaker's
appointment today. I'd wanted to take her out for drinks, as I
thought she might be lonely, but she said she couldn't make

it because of that. I can't reach her, I don't know what dressmaker, or where. I'll try her again now, at home, if I may." He went to the telephone, dialed, and stood listening; Maeve could hear the unanswered double ring.

Tom gave up only after a full minute. "She's probably let the staff go for the weekend, nobody— Perhaps you'd know about her dressmaker?"

"No, actually I haven't seen Lois since dinner the other night."

"You haven't?" He sounded startled. "But I'm sure I heard her tell Edwin that—" He stopped; his face closed.

That Lois was going to visit her sister-in-law.

Fen: "She looks very much to me like a woman in love."

It had crossed her mind, more than once, that Tom Gaymere might be Lois's new, secret love. There was something about his face when he said her name—but, apparently, she had the wrong man.

"Do you think you should go to the police?"

"That's what I'd hoped to get Fen's ideas on. If Edwin is on some perfectly legitimate, if mysterious, detour, and I raise the alarm and send the police in hot pursuit, he will take me out and stand me in front of the Bank of England and publicly strip me of my epaulets to the roll of drums."

"I don't suppose the Japanese airlines men can have gotten the wrong day?"

"No. I called his secretary at home, today's right."

In spite of his worried face, it all seemed quite unreal. The idea of anyone's interfering with Edwin's well-laid, indeed inexorable, plans was outrageous. The idea of anyone *taking* him, the chairman of Greatorex, Ltd., who used people, used money, used power, with cold magnificent skill, was ludicrous.

"But I still don't know," Tom was saying. "The car bomb the other night, and the threats, and the letters, that incendiary column of his—and Trann at his side like a great yellow-eyed dangerous dog, ready to go straight for someone's jugular—"

A key in the lock, thank heavens. An almighty barking and frisking about Fen by Mac; Fen was already his god, his hero, Alan Fort at least temporarily dismissed from the summit of his affections. Fen kissed his wife lightly and shook Tom's hand.

"Hello, Tom. Maeve, come upstairs with me for a minute. . . . There's something I have to attend to right away."

In the blue and white bedroom, he took her in his arms and kissed her properly. "It's been at me ever since I left you, I never told you, how frightful about Lafarge's dying, he was a good poet, too. . . ."

"It wasn't spoken, Fen, but it was in your eyes, or your nerve ends, which I can more or less feel."

"I know. God help me if I ever try to keep anything from you."

"And vice versa. But now—trouble, I'm afraid. This time on your side of the family."

"Of course the police will have to be notified," Fen said. "About Edwin, anyway. Leave out Lois for the moment."

Tom Gaymere had repeated his story to him, filling in the gaps. Edwin, driven by Trann in the Bentley, had left his house at nine o'clock. The drive to Hildegrave House in Surrey usually took about an hour and a half. His car was equipped with a telephone and he could have called ahead to the house in the event of any delay on the road, an accident, a blockage, a detour.

The housekeeper had finally, distractedly, served lunch to the two Japanese—"They never stopped looking at their watches, Mr. Gaymere, never, they drove me wild"—at 1:30, and then called Tom again. He had telephoned everybody he could think of, looking, in the meantime, for Lois, calling the Belgravia house in between his other, Edwin-hunting calls. Then he had driven over in his car to find Fen.

"Once you start thinking about who could be after Edwin, you get a little unnerved," Tom said. "Yes, thanks, Fen, I will have another. In addition to the Irish affair, he has a good many personal and, or, business enemies. There may have been some reason why some person or group didn't want this airlines deal to go through—"

"That's why we need the police, we can't just stand around and wonder what happened in which little lane after they left the main road," Fen said. "I'll call them, shall I?"

"No," Tom said. "I won't hide behind your—trousers. I will, right away."

"You stay here, then, if you will, and wait for them. I'm going over to Lois's—Maeve, will you come with me?—and see if she's back, she may be napping or something, the telephone turned off—"

She had given him a key to the Gaymere house three years

ago, for some reason he had forgotten; it still lay in the corner
of the center drawer of the lacquered desk in the hall.

In the taxi, he turned to Maeve. "If you were in love and
your husband left town, where would *you* be tempted to go?"

"To him, I suppose," she said, not liking the question or the
answer. "Provided there wasn't a wife on the premises, as there
well may be."

"I don't believe in her dressmaker. She's much too impatient
for that kind of thing, hem chalks and pins, turn around, dear.
She always has to leave a note on the hall table for Edwin,
saying exactly where she can be reached any time he wants
her. . . . It's probably a coverup for meeting this man of hers.
With the police about to flood the scene, as I'm sure they will,
there would be hell to pay if she was found with him, or
something found out about the two of them—"

As he turned the key in the lock, she held his arm tightly.

"You don't think there'd be anyone . . . waiting, in the
house? For her, something going to happen to her, too?"

"That's one reason why we're here. Keep behind me."

Silence, absolute. A scent of irises, strong and sweet, from
the huge white and yellow arrangement on the Louis XV table.
There was no note from Lois. They went quickly through the
empty, beautiful double drawing room, Edwin's library, the
dining room, the great shining kitchen. Then, up the stairs;
Fen purposefully led the way to Lois's bedroom. All pale,
gardeny, flowers everywhere, on the walls, the bedspread, and
the great tented canopy, the quilted chairs by the fireplace.
Hanging baskets of fuchsia and begonia in the windows, masses
of white marguerite on the hearth. The air slightly damp, and
fresh, and wholly private.

"You are to be completely ruthless," Fen said. "Just remember it's in a good cause. If she is with him, she has to be
found, and warned. Where would you hide anything from me,
something you'd die if I found out about but still couldn't bear
to throw away? Come on, Maeve, and hurry."

Fingers shrinking from the task, she went through drawers,
under scented stacks of the myriad things well-off and well-
turned-out women place in them. The dressing table, the writing
desk. The closets that ran the full length of the room, oval
panels of mirror set into them. How frightful to have that many
clothes, shoes, *things* to see to, but of course Lois Gaymere
wouldn't have to do it, that would be her maid's job—

"Do you, by the way, know her maid's name, and where she can be reached? Perhaps she's in on the secret—"

"No, a good idea, but I don't know a thing about her."

With a keen professional eye, she went through the labels on suits, coats, dresses, at-home clothes. Good London stores, Harrods, Jaeger, Liberty; British and French couture houses; not an unlabeled garment, to suggest a dressmaker, in the lot.

Eleven handbags to go through, six evening bags, hat and glove boxes.

Nothing. Not a note or letter or scribbled line on a bit of paper, not a menu or theater ticket stub affectionately cherished. She kept glancing at the open door, expecting to see an enraged blue-eyed dark-haired woman. Fen stood restlessly by the fireplace.

"I find myself hoping to God she's with him now. . . ."

"Fen, she could be in any one of a hundred places. This morning I was on my way to the Royal Festival Hall and wound up at the Speakers' Corner in Hyde Park. A gallery, drinks with someone, or just walking about—"

"Why would she give Tom this dressmaker story, then, if she was free for the afternoon? She's fond of him, he's a good friend of hers. She trusts him."

"Well, she'd hardly tell him, trust him or not, that she was off to meet her lover—"

"You forgot her telephone book. Here, I'll look." Maeve came over to scan it with him. Untidily kept, full names, nicknames—Nikki, Pots, Ved—initials, hairdresser, florist, the grouped numerals for ordering her daily life.

"You'd better look over her sitting room, just to be sure—"

A small room, books and a spinet piano, a little fireplace tiled in white.

"It would take a week to shake out every book," she called.

"Forget it, we haven't got a week."

"And now," Maeve said, coming back to the bedroom, looking at his troubled face, "what?"

"I don't know. Wait, I suppose—the hardest thing."

He went to the window and looked out as if he was expecting to see Lois, at any minute, turn in at the gate in the wrought-iron railing.

She cast a last glance around the room—had she missed anything? After all, this was to help Lois, not to pry and to spy. She went to the fragile porcelain mug on the writing desk, fingered through pens and pencils, a tiny solid gold ruler, a few rubber bands, found with her fingers, behind a gold pencil, a slim smooth engraved object, flicked her eye over it, took it out of the cup and dropped it in her pocket in a process of thought and action so fast she was hardly aware of its registering at all, and said, to his back, "Hadn't we better go home to the mews? She may have called there, wanting you—"

Had he seen her quick instinctive gesture, reflected in the window glass? She was sure he hadn't; the day outside, at a little before six, was still bright, late sun slanting through the plane trees to repattern the garlanded Aubusson carpet with floating leaf shapes. There were no lamps on, to make mirrors of the windowpanes against an outer dark.

TEN

"You're an excellent blusher, and now, I see, a blancher as well," Fen said, coming over to her from his place by the window. "What happened just now to take all your color away? Did you think of something, or hear a noise I didn't?"

The joy of being so close that your mind could be read had, she discovered for the second time in a few days, its drawbacks.

"It's just that I kept seeing Lois suddenly appearing at the door, watching this invasion. It might be a little hard to explain as she didn't admit anything even to you about a man—"

"Come on, then, we've done everything here I can think of, we'll go, but I'd risk her rage gladly if only she would walk in."

She wasn't, she told herself, dissembling; the little object could mean nothing and less than nothing.

They went around the corner into Belgrave Square and found a taxi right away. Down the immaculate and now twilit creaminess of Eaton Place, into Cavendish Place, and then into the whirl of traffic around Sloane Square.

The little, five-inch-long cylinder, narrowing and flattening at one end, was of old, thin silver, delicately engraved in a worn pattern of tiny ivy leaves.

She had seen it often, holding a cigarette, between Desmond's knuckles, his forefinger and second finger, while his thumb pressed thoughtfully into his cheek. The cigarette holder had presented itself to her notice, on and off, for years.

"I found it on the beach," he had told her, "where somebody no doubt in the flights of passion had forgotten all about it. I think it looks quite ancestral, don't you? It even, by some turn of fortune, has my initials engraved on the mouthpiece, see, D.B."

He had often left it behind, at her apartment on the top floor of Brenda's Merrion Square house. She always conscientiously returned his ancestral possession to him.

"You're quiet," Fen said, looking at her closely.

"Just thinking . . ."

Into the King's Road, now, demurely and handsomely residential here, with its green oblongs of grass and trees in the center, its pale house fronts, before it burst into its Western aspect of coffee bars and shops and stores, boutiques and pubs, kaleidoscopic crowds.

He could have been at a party, at some time, at the Gaymeres'. Michael Bye, handsome, golden, and not obviously and legally attached to anyone, went everywhere.

Lois could have picked up the cigarette holder, seen it as old and of some value, put it away carelessly in her porcelain cup—displaying no obvious attempt to hide it—in case someone called up and asked about it. He probably wouldn't have known exactly where he left it; he was always surprised and pleased when she found it behind a sofa cushion or on the edge of the kitchen counter. "I thought this time I'd said a final farewell to it, it could have been left in a dozen places yesterday."

There certainly wasn't enough to go on to assume that there was any kind of real connection between him and Lois. There certainly was a sound reason for withholding this discovery from Fen. He might very possibly leap to conclusions and regard the silver holder as a five-inch stick of dynamite. Desmond Byrne, he would think. He would say, Lois's lover. Lois's lover *too*.

She didn't like to imagine how his face would look.

". . . just brooding," she continued obliquely, "about Lois, I suppose there are worse things, if anything did happen to

Edwin or will happen, than a pair of kindly arms somewhere—"

"It usually involves more than kindly arms, Maeve. And Edwin may be intact, up to some maneuver of his own, he'd think nothing of standing up the whole Japanese nation to gain some particular end—and there's Trann, who may have assistant police dogs at his command to track down wandering wives, she could get herself into a horrible mess."

The police had been there and gone when their taxi reached 11 Polperry Mews. Tom was waiting for them.

"Two men, one of them an inspector, I must say they're efficient, quick, right to the point. I said there was a chance, in the remote possibility of his having been taken, abducted, that they'd, whoever did it, get in touch with me as I'm his nearest relative, but I don't know how these things go. I've never—"

He was told that he was under no circumstances to get in touch with the press, or to give out any information if the press called on him. They would handle that end of it if and when it was necessary.

They had then wanted to know what route Gaymere's car usually took, going down to Surrey; they would of course have the license number and description of the car at their fingertips. They had wanted to know where and how Tom had spent his day, and if he had been in communication all afternoon with his own office and residence to see if there had been any written or telephoned message for him; there hadn't been. And Mr. Fenway Vaughan and Mrs. Vaughan—how, mildly and politely asked, had they spent *their* day, did he know? They had wanted very badly to find and talk to Lois Gaymere.

"I didn't tell them she's disappeared, which in any case I'm sure she hasn't, but I said she was a bit of a butterfly, lots of engagements, they were going direct to her house and told me to have her get in touch with them in case she—"

"I think everybody had better sit down," Fen said carefully. "It's not a crisis yet, they may turn up something in an hour or so, and Lois may call at any minute. We will have one very no-nonsense drink, and then, Maeve, if you will get us something to eat—"

Maeve carried her drink into the kitchen, the cigarette holder all but burning a hole in her pocket. She took it out and examined it. The silver was lined with the thinnest shell of delicate dark wood, to keep it from heating up, she supposed. Yes, D.B.

engraved on the mouthpiece. Left behind at a party by that attractive writer, Michael Bye. But not a clue, even in the initials, to let Lois know to which of her guests it belonged.

"Where would you hide something from me, Maeve, something you'd die if I found out about?" A small matter, to consider later. Perhaps, ruthlessly, just throw the thing away.

The knocker was lifted and fell heavily against the door while she was trimming the lamb chops. It was the start of the time when the small everyday commotion of the doorbell, the knocker, the telephone were sounds to be feared.

Something kept her in the kitchen, intent on the chops.

Fen came in with a large white-ribboned white straw basket piled high with fruit, ripe apricots and mangoes, melons of so rare a variety she had never even seen them before, peaches and grapes and figs.

"Just ordinary everyday bad news," he said from the door. "Not big bad news. Shall I read you his note?"

"Yes, I must put these in—" Virtuous domestic bustle, turn on the broiler, take the tomatoes out of the boiling water and skin them for the salad.

"All my love, and then . . . something in Gaelic, I think—and of course—darling, D. What exactly does it say?"

". . . hard to translate literally, something like, I kneel and kiss your fruited mouth . . ."

"Or worse," he said. "You're probably being tactful—if this keeps up, as it seems very likely to, you must teach me Gaelic."

The tone of his voice was not encouraging.

He came over to her, gave her a long look, said, "Would you mind putting down that tomato for a minute? I must just kiss your fruited mouth, to reassure myself that—"

The knocker sounded again.

ELEVEN

"The police, for you, Maeve," Tom Gaymere said with gentle politeness. "I asked of course if it was about Edwin, and he said no. Can I mind the chops for you? I'm a good hand with a chop."

Fen went with her, through the dining room and into the hall. Not one intelligent or coherent thought occurred to her during this short trip.

"Mrs. Vaughan? I'm Detective-Sergeant Vesey. And is this Mr. Vaughan?"

Detective-Sergeant Vesey was a short stocky man with an overlarge head, thick brown hair, and the drooping hazel gaze of a beagle. He had spent a long and not very rewarding day asking questions about the Blessed Union. He had been made aware that this very house had just been visited on another matter that at the moment loomed far larger, a mislaid millionaire, a pillar of the United Kingdom's world of finance.

There had been two telephone calls to New Scotland Yard about the woman residing at 11 Polperry Mews. One was from an enraged cook who worked at Number 9. Coming home, late, from her evening out, she had seen the scroll on the door of the Fort house and some time during the morning had heard on her radio that the Blessed Union might conceivably be concerned not with peace and love but with guns and ammunition. She had lost a son in the British Army, in a street riot in Belfast. "There's a red-headed Irishwoman staying in that house—I've heard her talking to the poodle. Not an English voice at all."

The other call had been anonymous. A man, a low harsh voice, according to the report radioed to Vesey. "If it's Byrne you're asking questions about, there's a friend of his, a woman who's besotted with him and he about her. . . ."

The word "besotted" did not seem to fit the slender pale woman with the dark red hair and clear mossy green eyes who faced him so quietly, her hand in her husband's.

"Shall we go in and sit down?" she asked.

"I'd prefer to see you alone, Mrs. Vaughan."

"Sorry, impossible," Fen said.

Although his presence, so close beside her, was enormously comforting, Maeve for a moment was sorry, too.

Vesey shrugged and gave in. He sat uncomfortably on a lavender velvet bergère, notebook in hand. Maeve sat opposite him on the apricot sofa, Fen long-leggedly arranged half off and half on the arm of it, his hand at the side of her far shoulder, watchful, protective.

"We're looking into an organization called the Blessed Union. Are you a contributing member of this group, Mrs. Vaughan?"

"No. I am not." Mild. Eyes composedly meeting his.

"We got a report of a notice on your door here, that you'd given them a hundred pounds—"

"Wait a minute," Fen said, above her head; she felt his voice vibrating, near, over the troubled pounding of her heart. "We both live here for the time being. Why aren't you asking me if *I'm* a contributor?"

"We received several calls, Mr. Vaughan, one specifically mentioned Mrs. Vaughan. You're an American?"

"Yes. So, by the way, is my wife."

Vesey, whose wife had just left him, thought wearily, handsome chap, why on earth would she be besotted about another man? If, that is, the call wasn't plain, all too common, malice on someone's part.

"I can only assume," Maeve said, "that someone tacked the notice to our door as a joke, which I see now has badly misfired."

"Do you know a Mr. Desmond Byrne?"

"Yes."

She felt rather than saw the tensing of Fen's hand on the back of the sofa near her shoulder.

"We've been told that he's associated with this group. Do you know of any such association?"

"No."

What, if anything, had she ever told Fen about Desmond and the Blessed Union? His breathing sounded stilled, perhaps momentarily stopped and held—she remembered saying that Cooley, crudely soliciting funds from Fen at his office, was Desmond's creature.

"How long have you known Mr. Byrne?"

"Nine . . . ten years."

"Intimately?" Vesey thought he had better reword this. "Quite well, that is?"

"Very well."

"And you can state categorically that as far as you know he has nothing, nothing whatever, to do with the Blessed Union?"

"Yes. I can."

The betraying color swept her face but her eyes were steady. Something strange here, Vesey thought, she and this man—there was an almost audible crackle of electricity between them, of emotional and physical involvement so strong as to be disturbing to him.

But then, his wife had clear eyes, and had kissed him goodbye he thought quite lovingly the morning of the day she left him.

He looked at Maeve silently until her color receded. He stood up.

"Thank you, Mrs. Vaughan, for the moment we must take your word for it, a very old friend . . . where can we get in touch with Mr. Byrne? Nobody seems to have an address for him."

"I have no idea. I haven't one for him, either."

"I'll see myself out—"

"Just a moment and by the way, Detective-Sergeant—" Fen, very much disliking the scene, was entertained nevertheless by the sound of her voice, usually so soft. Bravery now, probably.

But with an unmistakable hint of the Waterford crystal chandeliers tinkling overhead, the avenue of limes, the light crack of a riding crop on the flank of a fine fast mare. . . . "Who informed you that I was a friend of Mr. Byrne's?"

It had just occurred to her that he might have a police record—horrible thought—and that she might be a part of it. Maeve Devlin, spinster, known associate of Desmond Byrne—

"A man called. No identity given."

They listened to the door closing behind him.

A faint clanking of silver from the dining room; Tom must be setting the table. Maeve got up from the sofa.

"The chops are probably ruined—"

Fen caught her shoulder.

"Were you lying to him?"

"Yes."

"You're surprisingly good at it. Always the best technique in these cases, don't embroider, say very little but say it quietly and firmly. . . ." He studied her face expressionlessly. "Why, Maeve? Or is that a silly question?"

"Paying off an old debt, or some of it. He saved my life, once." She told him about it in short dry syllables. She was shaken and felt raw and soiled. "He called me up and demanded this kind of payment, Fen. I thought in ways it was the least I could do. I'm sorry you had to be a spectator to my being turned inside out."

"For your life, I'm in his debt too," Fen said slowly. "It won't make me a friend of his, but—no, Officer, I know of no connection whatever of Byrne with this outfit, a man named Cooley never called on me, I never heard of Byrne's man Cooley as a matter of fact. . . ."

"I hate you to be dragged into this."

"But I am, aren't I?" Fen asked. "What choice do I have, Maeve?"

She felt an awful chill. Love and trust possibly eroding even while it was being volunteered, immediately and without question.

"Aren't *you* going to ask me about the connection—that bloody Union?"

"No. I'd feel more comfortable staying with my own assumptions but not having hard facts in hand, to have to deny."

"One thing you must hear. I think the guns theory is nonsense.

Material for a good bone-rattling hate-making column. If I believed there was anything to it, I wouldn't go along with this, for any reason whatever."

Would he ever, wholly, believe her, about anything, again?

Angered at her feeling of having been shamed, under his gaze, of having her honor forever in the balance, with him, she added crisply:

"As far as I can gather, it's mainly a money-making scheme sold to gullible people who should know better. Possibly no worse in any way than some of your brother-in-law's ventures."

From the door, Tom said, "I'm afraid the chops are getting a bit chilly, shall we eat them anyway? I've finished fixing the salad and it looks most untidy. I'm going to take a minute to ring the house again and see if Lois is there—"

Coming back, he said, "No one. Nothing."

They sat down at the table, carefully ingesting food they could not taste.

Tom left after drinking his coffee and eating a ripe apricot Maeve pressed on him; the other two did not touch the fruit.

He had a flat in Millbank, on Lord North Street. "I'll sit there and listen for the telephone or the doorbell, I suppose," he said a little dolefully. "You two are reassuring company, but I must get to my post. There might even be someone, some time in the night, wanting to see me—" He visibly regarded this last idea without enthusiasm.

"Call here anytime," Fen said. "I'll be up."

Mrs. Gossamer notwithstanding, Maeve occupied herself with doing the dishes, stretching the task, drying and polishing airy crystal and heavy antique silver and Royal Doulton.

At nine, Fen, who had been trying unsuccessfully to read, said he'd take Mac and tour the pubs in the Gaymeres' immediate neighborhood. "Lois might have run across people she knows, she often goes to the Grenadier in Wilton Row, and then there's another one, I forget the name. I hate to leave you here but someone has to listen for the phone."

"Don't be too long, please . . ."

To the large worry about Lois, and Edwin, had been added, for him, the bitter aftertaste of her police interview. Lovely wedding trip for Fen she and Desmond had managed, between them. Whose unkind tongue had talked to Scotland Yard about her? Someone from the mews, obviously, who had seen the scroll. And someone else pointing out that she knew Desmond Byrne.

Desmond himself? One of his Union men? Ridiculous thought, or perhaps not at all ridiculous. Chapter six, paragraph one, in Desmond's Michael Bye plot about the three of them. What quicker way to get her whitewash of him than to send the police directly to her through an anonymous call?

Fen was gone a long time. She could imagine his relief at moving, striding, actively looking for someone, not waiting for the silence to be pealed awake. He came back at a little before eleven, bringing, for her, a bottle of lager.

"Drink this down and then I'm going to see you off to bed, Maeve, you look tired."

"What will you do?"

"Stay up . . ."

"In the bedroom, then, please?"

She didn't want to be alone or have him alone in his vigil; and there was still something wrong between them, although they were pleasant and polite to each other.

"If the reading light won't keep you awake . . ."

She said it wouldn't; and didn't say only the sense of their not being in perfect harmony would do that.

He watched her as she came back from the bathroom in her nightgown, thin creamy Mexican cotton wrapped and held in slender Grecian bands encircling her ribs and narrow waist. Her hair spilled softly; her face was very pale.

"Even distress becomes you," he said. He went over and sat down on the bed beside her and took her hand.

"After Vesey went off, you asked me a question I didn't answer."

"What question? I don't remember—"

"You didn't say it aloud. But you said— You caught me lying, will you ever believe me again?"

He lifted the hand and kissed it. "I still can't believe you'd ever lie to me about anything important to the two of us, Maeve."

Not a forthright "I don't believe." But a quite different "I still can't believe." . . .

He was fighting it, then, his uncertainty, but you couldn't fight something that didn't have an existence of its own, however shadowy.

She wanted to cry and didn't, but reached forward and caught his head between her hands and pulled it down against her breasts and kissed the dark hair, with gratitude and love and a little sadness. Then she said, "Just a minute, Fen, darling."

She got out of bed and walked to the closet, reached into the pocket of her ivory linen suit, took out the silver cigarette holder, crossed the room again, and handed it to him.

If he was trying so hard to trust her, she felt obligated to have nothing to hide from him.

"I didn't and don't think this means anything but after what you've just said—this is Desmond's cigarette holder. I found it in Lois's pencil cup, on her desk."

He rolled it thoughtfully between his fingers. "And what did you think about its being there?"

"He does a lot of partying and they entertain a lot, the Gaymeres. He was always leaving the thing behind. And there's nothing in the initials, in case she wanted to return it, to connect him with Michael Bye, or—"

Suddenly and effortlessly, his other pen name dropped into her mind from nowhere. Ian Bray.

"Or what?"

"Ian Bray is the second name he uses, another publishing house, I can't remember which now, it amuses him to be his different selves as and when he chooses—"

"But why keep this thing in her bedroom? And not downstairs, for Bellington to handle in case the owner came knocking at the door?"

"You'd be surprised at what women keep in pencil cups. They're very handy repositories."

"I know." He smiled suddenly. "I have someone's gold roll-on mascara case in mine, at home, I'll never know why or how it got there, in case you suddenly pounce upon it—"

Then he surprised her by saying, "You may be quite right about its meaning nothing, the idea of . . ." His voice faded; he gazed as at a distant unreal vision. "The idea of his being Lois's lover too . . . talk about taking in each other's washing! It's too much. . . . Well, simple enough. When she turns up, I can just ask her, are you sleeping with any of these three men? All of them, as I believe you described him, frightfully handsome." He got up and began to prowl the room. "Christ, I wish the phone would ring—I'll call Tom, anything's better than silence."

His partial dismissal of any amorous connection between Lois and Desmond had a peculiar effect on her mental processes. I'm just playing devil's advocate, she thought. Just, really, trying to occupy my mind, so as not to think of what possibly could be happening to his sister. . . .

She knew the effect, particularly on women who hadn't met him, when Desmond walked into a room, gold and blue and resplendent. His half-smile, denting his long taut cheeks, his intent gaze as he took a hand, and the close-up surprise of the freckles on his well-cut nose and high cheekbones; at one time, she too had thought the freckles disarming, endearing, and had found herself wanting to finger them—

His meeting with Lois needn't have been accidental, coincidental. He could have occupied himself with finding out all about the man who had pre-empted the woman he had arrogantly still considered, in spite of all evidence to the contrary, his own. He could have learned there was a sister, living in London, could have arranged to meet her. To hurt and get at Fen through his family, revenge himself in some way—

No, a fantasy, born of the midnight-pointing hands of the clock, the worry and the waiting, the weary thinking up of explanations that didn't hold water: Lois could be staying with a friend, didn't want to be alone in the empty Belgravia house. She could be out, driving, somewhere in the countryside, in her own car. She could be at a late party, having a marvelous time, not thinking about going home before three or four o'clock in the morning—

Tom had heard nothing.

She slept fitfully, often waking to see Fen stretched out in the chair by the window, Mac sprawled profoundly asleep at his feet. His tired, drawn face with the eyes making dark holes in it. . . .

"Fen, go to bed for an hour or so. I'll spell you, I've had lots of sleep."

"All right, one hour . . ." He had been asleep for only ten minutes when the telephone rang. He waked instantly and took the receiver from her hand.

"They've called," Tom Gaymere said. "They have Edwin and Lois. They say they're safe and well. *Safe*, strange word, now that I—they say they'll be in communication with us shortly—"

"Tom." Fen's voice was patient. "Who is 'they'?"

"Well, actually, just the one voice, of course. Irish accent, young, soft, quite pleasant as a matter of fact. He said 'tarms' . . . I'd be hearing shortly about the tarms of their release.''

"And he called just now?"

"No. Half an hour ago exactly. He said I was to wait half an hour before I called any interested parties. He said there was a man outside in the street watching the windows of my flat, I'm on the second floor here, and that I was to leave the lights on and draw back the curtains so I could be seen. He said the man had a grenade, and would throw it if I was seen to pick up the telephone. There's just the one instrument here, at a table near the window. I must say these people are very thorough. . . . I waited, of course."

"Did you see anyone outside?"

"I didn't want to go near the window," Tom said. "It was a rather bad half hour, there are lots of other people peacefully asleep in this house. I'm going to call the police now and go to bed and I suggest you do the same, sleep, that is. He said it would be at the very least twenty-four hours before"—he sighed heavily—"we're told the tarms."

TWELVE

Ian darling, come and get me. You can find me, you can do anything, Ian, you wouldn't let anyone—

Childish of her to take shelter in arms that weren't there, repeat his name in her head like a charm to finger for secret comfort.

But it wasn't quite daylight. The small barred window high in the wall across the room was getting to be a clear purple. He wouldn't even know, yet. Perhaps wouldn't for two or three days, assuming she would be in Surrey, at Hildegrave House, with Edwin.

But, try thinking—difficult with her head aching so badly, at the back, where she had been struck. She would not arrive at Hildegrave House when expected, and Edwin would make a great fuss with the right people and she would be in all the newspapers. Unless, for some reason of his own, having to do with business in hand, Edwin wouldn't want her disappearance known.

The elasticized bandage about her mouth was tight; her dry

lips burned under it, and it was fastened behind her head just
where it throbbed. She rolled her head on the pillow and looked
at the man sitting on the straight chair next to her. There was
a small table beside him. On it were a paper cup, a pack of
cigarettes, a lighter, and a large greasily shining black gun.

He could be in his middle twenties, raw pink amiable face,
thatchy red hair, bright blue eyes, two teeth missing at the left
side of his half-open mouth, one above, one below. Tan cotton
shirt and trousers. He had taken off his tan cap.

When—waking from a deep sleep a little earlier, she had
started to scream and found she couldn't, tried to struggle
upright and found she couldn't do that either because she was
tied to the narrow bed—she had sensed and then seen him
there, her first feeling had been one of dazed and instant relief.
It wasn't, after all, Trann who was in charge of her.

"You may call me"—hard delicate lips a few inches away
from her own—"Michael, or Ian. Under either or both names,
I think I am going to adore you."

"Oh, Ian I think. It suits you better and besides there's a
man I hate, named Trann, whose first name is Michael."

They had met at a party at Elissa's, the night in early May
when Edwin had gone off to a conference in Paris.

"Lois dear"—Lois had arrived a little early and was combing her hair, Elissa watching her—"I'm about to expose you
deliberately to a shattering man. Are you in the mood?"

Thinking of her empty flowery house, and that morning, her
questioning and perhaps empty heart—"Do I love him?"—Lois
had said gaily, "Yes, why not?"

"It's time and more than time, for you, for a lover."

"I'm not a book of yours, Elissa."

"Edwin isn't a very interesting chronicle, either, except for
his funds, I mean, really, darling—"

"If he's so shattering, how is it you're ready to hand him
over?"

"There's a little matter of a man, a peer, I think perhaps I
will return to discretion while we see what happens next."

"You're over Fen, then?"

"Not at all, but for the moment I assume his attentions are
otherwise occupied, we must wait for the pre- and post-wedding
ardors to burn themselves out, and I am after all permanently
associated with him on a nice, serene business basis."

". . . Michael Bye, the thriller writer, Lois Gaymere. Hello, Peter dear, Lois, surely you've met Peter Collins, he's Michael's agent."

She hadn't seen a man so unselfconsciously and effortlessly take over a room since she had last watched her own brother walk through a doorway.

"I haven't read you, but I promise I will," Lois said.

His fingertips very lightly touched her wrist.

"Come along right now, and read me."

She knew she looked something approaching her best, deliberately creamy pale, very little makeup, arms and shoulders bare. Dark hair caught back and held at the nape of her neck with a spray of diamonds, black silk fringed thirties dress, the fringe swinging to the slightest movement; she shimmered.

The two of them had swiftly broken loose from the group in the center of the room and gone with their drinks to an open window in a dim and relatively deserted corner. She found herself astonished by the sheer, male blaze of him.

His height and carriage made all the other men there look shriveled, or dumpy, or not correctly formed. His clothing made them look rumpled and hastily thrown together.

After twenty minutes, he had said, "Elissa's watching closely. You were at first fascinated and so was I, but I've said something that has annoyed you, we've fallen out about politics or your liking cats and my hating them. Flounce away, Lois, do."

Her eyes locked in his, she had said anxiously, "But—"

"I like a private life and I expect you do too. Talk nicely to other people now, especially men. I will talk nicely to other people, especially women, and leave reasonably soon. I will meet you, both of us arriving separately, at ten o'clock at the Devonshire Arms, just off the Hogarth cloverleaf in Chiswick."

"That's *miles* out . . ."

"Privacy, I think I said." An order; but one thrilling in its promise. "Look at your watch, Lois, and see that we are both in exact time with each other."

Light from a nearby lamp caught his brassy golden hair. She felt immersed in the blue shine of his eyes, bottomless azure.

"We will agree to disagree, Mr. Bye," she said clearly and coldly—well overheard by the couple standing a few feet from them, overheard, even, by Elissa—and she moved away, head high, holding close to her a new, a forgotten, a wonderful soft warmth.

Yesterday, she had followed her usual procedure: gotten out of the taxi in front of Lambeth Palace, wandered a bit in the old garden at the side with its roses and time-dark mausoleums and worn gravestones, then walked leisurely four blocks, two left, two south, into mildly shabby Caudle Street. At the side of a plate-glass window, displaying a silver pants suit and a silver droop-brimmed hat, she opened a green door. Inside the small entrance hall, the door to the left led into MARCIE, DRESSMAKER.. The flight of stairs went straight up to the surprisingly handsome and roomy flat on the first floor front.

Starting to undress her, tenderly and expertly, he said, "Relax, I've been watching, no one at all in the street except an old woman with a string bag of cabbages, why do you worry so about Trann, and anyway, didn't you say he'd be out of town?"

"It's just the way he looks at me whenever I've been with you, and smiles to himself, you have no idea how ghastly—"

"He can't know anything, and if he ever does, I'll handle him, don't worry."

She had just returned to the empty Belgravia house when she saw the van turn in to the gravel drive between pillars and go under the archway at the side of the house to the back. The kitchen doorbell rang.

Packages being delivered for her, or Edwin; she had ordered six cashmere sweaters yesterday from Liberty.

She went into the kitchen and opened the door. She took no particular notice of the delivery man. A big, brown box, a name unfamiliar to her, something for Edwin, then—

She was turning away to get her handbag and find a tip for the man when she was struck, with something at once soft and hard, at the back of the head.

As the immaculate waxed white linoleum soared up to meet her, the last thought she remembered was, Trann, Trann, what are you going to do to me . . . ?

The man on the straight chair gazed into her dark blue eyes and smiled.

"Well, that was a good long sleep you had, of course helped on a bit but nothing to do you any harm—"

He seemed strangely like a slightly uncouth young intern, watching over her as she slept.

"From the look of the light, we can expect a fine day." Soft voice, Irish, perfectly friendly. "Now, here's the position. Kidnapped is a hard word, just say we've taken you and are holding you while we ask for a few things in return for your safe and speedy delivery to your home and loved ones. No one's going to hurt you or put so much as a finger on you if you co-operate. Think of yourself as our guest, an honored one, indeed."

I.R.A., she could only assume; he probably wouldn't tell her, when her mouth was free to ask. Edwin with his "One Man's View," Edwin with his ambitions, Edwin with his car-bombed Gaymere House.

"We have your husband too," he said. "He's in another room, here. You'll be needing something to eat and drink and I'm going to unstrap and untie you and set you free as a bird. The only thing is, if you scream, or make a rush for the door, I'll shoot. Not you, mind, I wouldn't do that, but into the air, so, and the man with Gaymere will shoot him, sorry to say to kill. Do you agree to stay nice and quiet in this room?"

She nodded her head in earnest assent. Under the friendliness, she could sense the efficiency and watchfulness, sharp and ready as a knife's edge.

Hands keeping themselves fastidiously free of her body, except when he had to lift her head to undo the elasticized bandage, he removed her bonds. She sat up in an agony of relief, moved the muscles of her face, straightened her back, and stretched her arms.

"I'm Larry, ma'am, when you want to address me for any reason." He picked up the pistol and backed to the door, eyes steadily on her, opened it, and called merrily, "Breakfast for Mrs. Gaymere, if you please."

It came in ten minutes, handed in at the door by an invisible person. Thick brown bread and butter, a pot of strong hot tea, a slightly chipped white cup patterned with little blue flowers. All neatly arranged on a round tin tray, with a paper napkin someone had folded into a triangle. She ate and drank gratefully. He watched her with approval.

"Nothing like breaking the fast, is there, the way the word 'breakfast' came along to us . . . I'm glad to see you do justice to it."

"Where are we?" Lois asked. She was not at all frightened, physically. This was, in its way, a business deal like any other. Edwin, in whatever room he was being held, would of course cope with it as he coped with everything. He would hardly risk his own precious life by refusing to meet their demands. Or hers.

"That would be telling, wouldn't it? A long, long way from home is where you are but in good kind hands."

Ireland?

No way of pinning this room to any particular place or any special country. Old, flaking, plastered walls, a low ceiling, the one high barred window, a feeling of being partially below ground, in some kind of half-basement. Scarred wooden floors, the narrow tarnished brass bed made up with coarse white muslin sheets and a cheap white chenille spread. The straight chair, the little table, nothing else. Two doors, in opposite walls.

"Am I to be allowed to see my husband?"

"No, you're to be kept separate, I'm sorry to say, but you'll have the rest of your life in each other's arms, so—"

"What are they—what are you asking for, for our . . . ransom, I suppose you'd call it?"

"I myself like the word 'return' better. For your speedy and safe return. Don't concern yourself with the details, don't worry your head about them."

"May I get up and walk about?"

"Of course, we wouldn't want your circulation folding up on you. And just so you won't torture yourself wondering what's outside the window, here—"

He dragged the straight chair across the room and set it under the window. "I'll help you up, you'll be a bit unsteady on your legs."

A moving, breeze-fluttered vertical mass of green ivy, perhaps two feet away, growing on some wall. No earth, no sky, no texture of stone or brick, nothing to define what the ivy was growing on, or where.

"This door, here—" He opened the far door and waved delicately at the tiny bathroom revealed: sink, toilet, rough white towel and washcloth folded on the edge of the sink. "Your own private bath, used by nobody else here, it's unlocked, you see, unfortunately no window but a good strong light bulb, and there's the bit of mirror over the sink. Too bad you couldn't have packed a change of clothes but it wouldn't have done to give you proper notice, now would it?" He winked and smiled at her.

Lois found herself smiling back at him.

"Now, then, ma'am, do you read?"

"Read . . . ?"

"You'll have to have something to pass the time." Out of his pocket, he took a Georges Simenon paperback. "I was at this myself while you slept, it's an interesting class of story, you're welcome to it, they'll be relieving me soon so I can get my wink."

Lois thanked him, poured another cup of tea, propped the pillow against the brass headrail of the bed, and settled herself comfortably to read *The Fate of the Malous*.

PART
THREE

ONE

The police had evidently decided to open the dam, to the press, on the subject of the disappearance of Edwin Gaymere.

It was the morning's major story, in the newspapers and on television and radio, elbowing aside the trouble in the Mediterranean and the explosion late the afternoon before on a Thames excursion boat to Richmond, in which ten adults and two children had been seriously injured.

It was indeed a juicy story, with fascinating ramifications. The great black Bentley carrying the internationally known British financier, chairman of Greatorex, Ltd., and his secretary-bodyguard-chauffeur, Michael Trann, to a peaceful working weekend in the country—where was the car, and the two men in it? The waiting Japanese airlines men, still staying at Hildegrave House, in case it turned out to be some mysterious Western misunderstanding. The unanswered question, "Where is Mrs. Edwin Gaymere?" with her picture, a recent snapshot Tom had supplied, Lois enchanting in a wide-brimmed straw hat and floating flowered velvet-tied chiffon at a country garden

party. Had she too been, possibly, abducted, separately? She
had not accompanied her husband but was to go down to Surrey
today, by prearrangement, in her own car. This car, a white
Mercedes convertible, was now in the garage of the house in
Belgravia.

"Will anyone who saw this woman on Friday, at any time
after 9 A.M., please contact the London Metropolitan Police at
the following number . . . the police are particularly interested
in finding Mrs. Gaymere's dressmaker, with whom she is said
to have had an afternoon appointment."

Squads of men were still combing every inch of the various
routes the Bentley might have taken on the journey to Hildegrave House.

Television cameras roamed the grounds of the Gaymeres'
handsome country home, with its two hundred acres, its stables
and rose gardens and maze of ancient box, its great herbaceous
borders edging the "Long Walk" to the fountains at the front
of the terrace, a great clustered leap of bronze dolphins.

A history of Gaymere's rise to his present financial eminence
was detailed in the newspapers, the ambitious young man "of
yeoman stock" starting as a bank teller, "but, it must be added,
in his father's bank," and driving steadily and relentlessly on
to become the guiding light of a multi-billion diversified enter-
prise embracing twenty countries in both hemispheres. His
column, the threats and the letters, the bombing at Gaymere
House were richly rehashed.

There was no mention of the fact that Thomas Gaymere,
Edwin Gaymere's rather obscure younger brother, head of the
research department of Greatorex, had been contacted and informed that he would soon be told the terms of the release of
the Gaymeres.

"Why, Fen?" Maeve asked, as they sat drinking too much
coffee, the radio on, the newspapers open, the late May sun
shining in on their tired faces.

"I suppose so as not to scare them off before they say what
they want."

The press named no one and blamed no one, as yet. Its
coverage, however, of Gaymere's joustings with Irish extremists, was pointed.

"For which, for the kidnappers, read I.R.A.," Maeve said.
"Or, depending on one's degree of cynicism, anti-I.R.A., out
to make them look even more sinister, ruthless, all-powerful . . ."

"I wonder if you'd be so open-minded," Fen said, "if it was your own family. Brenda, say."

The sound of his voice brought a rush of color over her pallor.

"I see no reason to stop thinking just when you need your mind most," she said crisply. "And your brother-in-law, as Tom said, has a bundle of business enemies to his credit. I've thought, often, what a convenient cover-up political crime is for personal motives. You remember, he thought there might be some conflict in the airlines sale—"

"Anyone, anything, but the Irish," Fen said. "You needn't be so defensive. You are, after all, an American, Maeve." He added thoughtfully, "In some ways. In a few . . ."

The room was very quiet, all of a sudden. Maeve, tension gripping at her ribs again, said, "I'll take Mac out, I have to move about a little, do let's be nice to each other, Fen. I know how you're feeling—Lois . . ."

Sniff the roses, breathe in the soft sweet air, try to dismiss the recollection of his eyes, assessing her, a possible adversary or even an enemy. What—as his eyes had asked, in her apartment in New York, after Cooley had visited him—what after all do I really know about you, Maeve Devlin?

He was waiting for her, standing in the open doorway, as she came back up the mews with Mac.

"They've found Trann," he said. "He's dead."

Trann's body had been found deep in a woods running along the northwestern boundaries of Hildegrave House. He had been shot through the head, by a rifle, over one ear; the police had yet to calculate an approximation of the distance from which the shot had been fired, but it looked like the work of a trained marksman. Clean, accurate, and fatal; one bullet.

The Bentley was a few hundred feet away, on a grassy path which had been used by Mrs. Gaymere for riding her horse through the woods. The letters I.R.A. had been scrawled hastily, in red paint, on the car's front left-hand door.

Of Gaymere, there was no sign. There was blood on the front seat, where Trann had probably toppled when he had been shot, but no sign of violence in back. Gaymere's attaché case was there, on the gray velvet tufted upholstery, his dictating machine, his black homburg.

The police did not know yet if the crime had been committed on the road, and the car driven later into the woods; or if it had taken place in the seclusion of Gaymere's own private and personal grounds. It was the sheerest luck that discovered Trann to the gaze of a young sergeant; a ray of early sun striking through the almost impenetrable branches of an immensely tall fir tree whose silver-green skirts fell thickly, deep into the long grass at its base. The single, chance, and almost immediately shifting ray lit the gold of Trann's watchband, flared light at the puzzled sergeant, then took it away again.

Something, in under that tree? Yes, something.

Telling her about it, Fen went on, his voice almost calm, but talking far more rapidly than was normal for him, as if trying to keep up with his racing thoughts—"Of course, they would have had to kill Trann. He was armed, known by them to be armed, if they've done their homework—he's dangerous, and has only one function, a lethal one— But that doesn't mean anything has happened to Lois. Or Edwin. Without proof to offer, that they're alive, they'll be in trouble collecting whatever it is they want"—he drew a long breath—"wouldn't you say, Maeve?"

"Yes." She unleashed Mac and went into the house with him and put her arms around him. "Yes, Fen, I would."

On the BBC news, at noon, a taxi driver was reported as saying he had picked up a woman who looked like Lois Gaymere in front of Lambeth Palace at 6:10 and driven her to the address in Belgravia. She had looked, he said, quite well, as a matter of fact, very pretty, very happy, she and he had agreed what a pleasant afternoon it was, after the rain yesterday. . . .

"He brought her home a few minutes after six," Fen said. "We got there, when?—six-thirty or so. Where on earth did she go?"

"They told Tom they had her."

"Then they must have picked her up, right there, at home. Or a bluff on their part, maybe . . . she could be hiding somewhere, she's heard and—would she possibly have gone running to her man?"

"I can't imagine a woman doing anything so foolish, in a case like this the police would always go straight to the wife first, wouldn't they? She'd hardly like to set up the two of them as the object of a police search."

"Nothing. No one."

Tom Gaymere had fallen into a speech pattern that was to

punctuate the endless Saturday hours, when the house could not be left because of the telephone. He called them often, for a thin kind of comfort, as well as to keep them posted. "The police are about, with all kinds of peculiar equipment, but they're more or less invisible. I hope they won't discourage anybody trying to get a message to me. . . . I feel I'm in a plane over Heathrow, circling endlessly, and that I'm never going to land . . ."

"Maeve and I are on the same plane, Tom," Fen said. "Right across the aisle from you. I'm going to order a drink from the stewardess. I suggest you do the same."

At a little after four, the Vaughans received their share of police attention. Two polite men, one gray-haired, one blond, arrived, and separately interviewed Maeve and Fen. Their questions to each, later compared, were alike.

Had Mrs. Gaymere ever received any threats, did they know, or were they always directed against her husband? Were Mr. and Mrs. Gaymere happily married, as far as they, her brother and sister-in-law, knew? Yes, indeed, Maeve said. Oh, absolutely, Fen said. When had they last talked to Mrs. Gaymere? Days ago. Were they not, then, on friendly terms? Yes, very friendly, but we're here on a wedding trip and I have some business to do, for my firm, and Lois has a pretty well-filled life of her own. . . . No, no one has contacted us, we assume it will be Tom Gaymere they will talk to if and when they get around to it—there's the telephone now— Yes, of course we will get in touch with you, immediately, if we hear anything.

Tom, at eleven o'clock. They had called him, at 10:30, and told him to go to St. John's Church, a few blocks from his flat, where he would find a brown envelope thrust under the south door with just its edge protruding. He had done so.

The envelope had not been sent through the mail, but obviously deposited by hand.

Tom had asked the police if that meant the Gaymeres were somewhere nearby and had been told that this was not necessarily so; if a group of people was involved, the delivery to the church could have been prearranged with one of them.

The envelope contained a tape of Lois's voice which when played said, "I am well, and am being cared for comfortably. My husband is here in another room but I have not been allowed to see him, I am told he is well and comfortable too. I've been asked to say this tape is being made today, Saturday, at five o'clock, and the time is accurate, if my watch is right." Her voice sounded calm and clear.

It also contained an eight- by ten-inch sheet of white bond paper, specifying the terms of the Gaymeres' release. "Separate price tags," Tom said in a tired and breathless voice. For Gaymere, the freeing of two prisoners being held, awaiting trial, for arson and the resultant death by fire of two men and one woman, in Belfast: Jeremy O'Toole and Gerald Quaid. For his wife, a quarter of a million pounds. Tom was to be allowed twenty-four hours to get the sum in hand, and would then be notified as to what to do with it.

"Of course you're going ahead with it?" Fen asked.

"Of course." His next call, he said, would be to Greatorex's treasurer, Sir Roger Balt.

"The police are not getting in the way of . . . ?"

"They aren't talkative but they assure me their first concern is getting Lois and Edwin safely back, and I have no choice but to believe them. I do assure you, Fen, that she sounded fine, sounded herself, Lois is no actress as you know, she doesn't even tell a decent lie when the occasion arises. You'll want sleep, you must be exhausted, Maeve too, I know I am, I'm going to have whiskey and some aspirin after I talk to Balt, there's nothing more to be done tonight."

It couldn't have been a more unfortunate night for what might have been considered, under other circumstances, the relatively minor incident of the violets.

At some time around two o'clock in the morning, when, after hours while their exhausted bodies and minds simultaneously fought and wooed unconsciousness, they both finally slept, Fen was terrified awake by something that sailed in through the night-drifting ninon curtains and struck him full in the face, something soft, something damp.

Maeve waked to his stunned half-gulping half-swearing sound.

He switched on the bedside lamp and picked up, from where it lay on his chest, a great purple bunch of violets, rimmed with paper lace and fluted silver foil. The stems were neatly wired. A little note was tied with a string to the wire.

It said, "The young May moon is beaming, love, look out and see and think of me. Always, darling, D."

Fen stared at the flowers in his hand. The wire had scratched his cheekbone; a single drop of blood ran slowly down his face.

"Open a window, he climbs in," he said to the flowers. "Go out a door, you stumble over him."

The sound of his voice held her very still; hardly breathing.

"Always, darling, D. Christ, always and forever. He's become—and you by the way with him"—he had not yet even looked at her—"an appalling goddamned bore. I wish you had let me know what I was going to be in for. Perhaps, if you had—" He didn't finish the sentence. There was no need to.

He got out of bed and put on a robe. He came around the foot of the bed and carefully laid the bouquet on the table at her side of it. He still hadn't looked at her face.

He can't bear the sight of me—

She would have been happier if he had hurled the flowers into the fireplace.

He went to the window and leaned on the sill. A line of silver light edged his head and neck and shoulders, which were held very rigidly.

"Your moon, yes . . . I suppose he's well on his way, out of the mews," he said, not turning around. "And it doesn't matter now, anyway."

He went out of the room and across the hall. She heard the door of Alan Fort's own bedroom close behind him, not with the enraged slam that would have been somehow releasing, reassuring; but firmly, and quietly, and finally.

TWO

After the silence, and the pain, came anger. Helpful in its strange way, absorbing.

She knew that it had been his rage, however quiet, talking, taking over; the invaded, infuriated male. But now there seemed only one course open to her.

"—and you by the way with him, an appalling goddamned bore. I wish you had let me know—" I wouldn't have married you.

Halfway dressed, she hesitated. Go pound her fists on his door, call through the heavy wood paneling, Fen, I didn't ask for the flowers, I didn't ask for any of it, I don't know what it's all about—but if he didn't believe it anyway, what would saying it all over again prove?

She took her airlines carry-on case out of the closet and rolled in it silk jersey tunic and pants, which wouldn't wrinkle—yes, stop and take time to think of wrinkles when the walls are collapsing on you—underclothing, a robe and slippers. She put cosmetics and soap and toothpaste and toothbrush into the zipped waterproof pockets of the case.

I'm getting out of this car, thank you. I'm going home to mother. Ridiculous—

If he had only, just once, looked into her face. Found in her eyes the simple naked truth, her love.

It wasn't, after all, the sort of situation where you could apologize gracefully in the morning—I'm sorry I said what I said, I'm sorry I did what I did—and kiss and make up.

She hadn't said anything and hadn't done anything. There was no meeting ground at all, for them to stand on.

She remembered suddenly his cataloguing of his imperfections, after she had called Brenda in Dublin about him and about their going to marry each other. She had left out, among other things, he had told her, his extreme possessiveness and occasional horrible temper.

Harsh, to leave him with the big, bad business of Lois, in very obvious and open danger of her life, filling his sky.

But the matter of Lois was in the hands of Tom, and the police; their only role, hers and his, was waiting, waiting—

She could at least spare him, and herself, the rasp, the bruise, the maddening last-straw attentions of Desmond Byrne. And the remote but not dismissible possibility of lethal plans for Fen.

Raincoat, umbrella. She had four fifty-dollar traveler's checks in her wallet and about thirty-five pounds in cash. Fen made a point of seeing, always, that she had plenty of money in case of emergencies, in case, somehow, they got separated.

Mac, head on his paws outside the other bedroom door, rolled an eye at her as she went by, questioning but sleepy. In any case, his eye said, this was his proper place, as close to Fen's door as he could get, and here he would stay.

The stair carpet silenced her descending footsteps. She hoped a little, until she had safely closed the front door behind her and listened for its safety lock clicking into place, that there would be a commotion, a door opening, a voice calling down—

Perhaps he was already asleep. It was getting on for three o'clock now. He couldn't have had a total of more than two or three hours' sleep in two succeeding nights.

At the hall desk, she had stopped to scribble a note. "Fen, I'm off to a hotel for a bit to draw the scent away from you, at least one small thing you won't have to worry and bother about. I'm not sure at this hour where I'll land but after we've both slept I'll call you and tell you where I am." She hesitated and then signed it with the single initial, "M."

She had to walk all the way to the Royal Hospital Road before she found a taxi. The moonlit night, the emptiness, the silent houses and streets were not at all terrifying, as they would have been in New York; she felt quite safe.

When he picked her up, the taxi driver thought, Mmmmm, just tumbled out of some man's bed, but when she spoke he wasn't so sure, after all.

"I need a hotel, and it may turn out to be a bit complicated at this hour. We'll start with the Park Lane in Piccadilly." Calm voice, sober; a moneyed and leisured music to it, not English, probably not American, possibly Irish.

The yawning, formally dressed man at the reservations desk at the Park Lane was similarly soothed, in spite of the hour. Charming suit, gray-green linen, steady eyes and shining bare head, intonation pleasant and not used to asking favors. "I want a room for at least one night, possibly longer, have you anything for me?"

"Only a suite, madame, I'm afraid."

"That will do nicely."

A firm hand, signing the register card. Mrs. Fenway Vaughan, U.S. citizen, no matter how Fen regarded her. New York address. Passport number.

In the bedroom of her suite, she undressed, took one of the sleeping tablets that she turned to perhaps three times in any given year, and went to bed. Soon it would hit bottom and go to work, and she could stop thinking, twisting, turning from one side to the other . . .

Try, in the morning, to exchange the suite for a single room . . . it mightn't be long, a day or so, but she really hadn't any concrete plans for her immediate future, it was just that she had to find Desmond, deal with him . . . if it took longer, and if she really was on her own, there was money in New York, in her checking account, see American Express about it . . . call Mrs. Locket at Brenda's house, on the thin chance that she might be able or see fit to supply Desmond's whereabouts . . . try, first thing in the morning. Peter Collins again, as a start . . . ? She went down deep, into sleep.

When, sandy-eyed with the heavy sleep, she woke at ten o'clock and reached for the bed table telephone and dialed Alan

Fort's number, it was Elissa Field who answered.

"Maeve! I saw the papers when I was in Edinburgh and I rushed over this morning, without taking time to call, to see what comfort I could offer you both, Lois is a dear friend of mine, too—I was so sorry to find you'd left the house, earlier . . . d'you want Fen? He's right here beside me—"

Too bad. Neither of them, under the circumstances, could talk freely. She could imagine how Elissa would enjoy the ringing echoes of marital conflict.

"Maeve." The two syllables, low, in Fen's voice. Angry still? She couldn't tell.

"I'm at the Park Lane, suite forty-seven, they hadn't a single room, if I change rooms I'll let you know—that's all, I don't want to tie up the phone in case—"

"How long"—neutrally but then Elissa was at his elbow—"do you think you'll be out?"

"I'm not sure, there's nothing I can do now to help, about Lois, so I'm applying myself to my other errand. Say anything, I don't want to embarass you—say Brenda's in town and she's ill and I went to her—no, that's bad luck, just say I'm with my aunt, presumably she—Elissa—won't be there all day, anyway. I'll call you later. There are things I can't go into until you're alone . . . and if I can't reach you, call me here at the hotel and leave a message."

"I will expect you then"—still the quiet of rage, or another, controlled kind of firmness?—"toward the end of the day. Or, if you're not here by five or so, I will of course come and pick you up."

"We'll see. I hope to God you'll have had good news before that, and I'll at least mentally be keeping you company all day. Good-bye, Fen."

Good-bye. Good-bye. When had she said it last? So few times, since their marriage; it hadn't been a word they needed often. Yes, the last time had been where he had been going off to Cambridge to see his don; and he had come back three times from the door to kiss her.

"Sorry, Mrs. Vaughan," Peter Collins said. "He's revising two chapters in a hotel room somewhere, he won't tell even me where, you know how he is when he's revising, and how he hates it, or do you?"

Something in his voice embarrassed her. She wondered if

he knew about Desmond's pursuit of her, and fancied that now, however freshly married, she wanted him for personal, emotional reasons.

"Has he a deadline he's meeting? When will he . . . ?

"His own deadline. Which is long as he can stand banging away at the typewriter. He'll go twenty-four hours at a stretch, sometimes, fueled on Guinness, but then, you're probably familiar with his impetuous ways . . . When he surfaces, dear, I'll be in touch."

She called his stepmother, Genevieve, Brenda's sweet and scatter-brained cousin, in Donegal. "Maeve? . . . Lovely to hear your voice . . . No, I don't know where you can find him, he's drifting, you know, as he does, I don't think it's creditors, he makes quite good money at his books, I *am* so happy hearing you asking for him, there isn't anyone else for him but you, you know, never has been . . ."

"I'm married," Maeve said patiently. "To someone else, Genevieve. You remember—a bit more than two weeks ago?"

"Oh, yes, a man named Vaughan—bring him to see us, darling, do."

Someone, somewhere, must know where he was.

Peculiar, the short telephone conversation with Mrs. Locket in Dublin; but then Mrs. Locket was and always had been a peculiar woman.

The ringing went on for quite a long time. She could see in her mind the big silent house in the square, the telephone bell pealing through its high-ceilinged rooms with their white plaster work of lace and air. It would be dark, because when Brenda was away Mrs. Locket asserted her fierce proprietorship over the health and color of carpets and curtains and kept the shutters closed, the house blinded, except for her sitting room and bedroom off the kitchen.

The two maids, Rose and Eva, would have been sent home to Galway; Moore, the chauffeur-gardener, would also have been furloughed until Brenda's return.

"Hello!" Mrs. Locket finally demanded, from across the Irish Sea.

"It's Maeve, Mrs. Locket, I'm looking for Desmond, it's frightfully important, can you tell me where to find him?"

There was a long silence. Was she using it to down some of her ale, or was she considering something?

Then, harshly, "Why ever did you call *me?* Here? Tell me that, miss!"

Shades of the days when she had been interrogating an adolescent girl about who had eaten the last of the cinnamon cake, or did her Aunt Brenda know at what disgraceful hour she had come home last night?

"I called you there because that's usually where you are," Maeve said tartly. "And it was just on the off chance, but I knew you and he are such old friends that—"

There was a blanking, blotting sort of nonsound; as though Mrs. Locket had covered the mouthpiece of the receiver with the palm of her hand. Maeve hadn't been aware until then that her radio was playing, faintly, in the background; but the radio noises had now totally vanished.

"I haven't the remotest idea where Desmond Byrne is," Mrs. Locket said, coming back on. "If you'll tell me what it is you're so bound and determined to talk to him about—to see him about—I'll make a mental note and pass along the information when and if he's in touch with me, which could be weeks from now."

"Thank you, never mind," Maeve said.

"Thank you, never mind," Mrs. Locket mocked. "You've bugled me away from my lunch and no doubt by now it will be cold as stone and you'll pay good money for this call, but it's of no importance after all?"

"No, just an idea. Go have another bitter, Mrs. Locket."

The housekeeper, when she replaced the receiver, stood thinking. Chin lifted, she listened for any sounds from the top of the house. There were none. Only the ticking of the clock and the murmur of the footsteps going, almost inaudibly, up the great marble stairway carpeted in amethyst velvet.

She went into her bedroom, opened her handbag, got out her little black book, and with the lines deepened in her long face, dialed a London number.

THREE

It wasn't any special instinct that sent her to the Spread Eagle pub in Pimlico; but merely a severe scarcity of choices.

This is where it had all started, the feeling of Desmond hovering unseen, unnervingly nearby. The piano tinkling out "The Young May Moon."

She had certain quarrels with England, but none about that amiable and beneficent institution the English pub. She loved pubs, the sense of not being a woman alone, eyed and wondered about, but a person, allowed comfort and dignity as well as refreshment, among other people who shared the same blessings.

The Spread Eagle at a little after eleven in the morning made no concessions to the brisk, breezy, sunny morning outside. Its dusky curtains were drawn; there was the same glow of apricot light from the fringed silk shades, the subdued glimmer of the great square mahogany bar, the smoldering of the carnations on the black wallpaper. Smoke drifted, thin and blue, the pop music still thumped—the heart still beating—and the

identical group of four men near the wall opening, beyond
which stood the piano, played cards with midnight intentness.

She went to the bar and ordered a half pint of special bitter.
A pleasant-looking red-faced man in a cobalt-blue shirt drew
the ale for her.

"The man who plays the piano here," she said. "I forget his
name . . . ?"

"That would be Jimmy. Jimmy Doolan." His own accent
was Irish.

"He's a friend of a friend and I want to say hello and pass
along a greeting, do you think he'll be in?"

"He's usually in by twelve-thirty Sundays, go sit yourself
down by his piano and you can't miss him."

She took her bitter into the front room and sat on an end of
the tufted black banquette right next to the piano, and uncomfortably near the machine exuding the music.

There would be time, before he came, to call Fen and see
if he had heard anything. It was no part of her plan to keep
him in suspense, maliciously, as to where she was or what she
was doing.

"Is Elissa still with you?" she asked. Test the water with
your toe before you step in. . . .

"No, and did you find Desmond last night, when you ran
from me? I didn't think to ask this morning, couldn't, actually,
with her here. She did cook me a good breakfast."

"Fen," she said very quietly. "No—it's today that I'm looking
for him, Fen."

"The police have been here, wanting to talk to you. Apparently someone, it could only have been that Clyde woman at
dinner the other night, called them up about you. Failing your
presence, they wanted to know from me where you stay in
Ireland when you go there, who your friends and associates in
Dublin are— Oh, and they wanted a picture, a photograph of
you. I said I didn't have one." His voice sounded hard; but
she didn't know if it was anger directed at the police questioning
or at her, the cause of it.

"But this is insane."

"From their point of view, perhaps not, you're closely con-
nected with the family now, the jargon they got from Angela
Clyde was all about bombs, and your hating the British Army,
and of course there are the strong bonds with Ireland—you'd
have a way of knowing his comings and goings, Edwin's, and

Lois's too—if you wanted to pass along the information to interested people . . .".

From her, absolute silence.

"I'm only telling you what *they* are probably thinking, not what I think," Fen said. A conversation in a dream. It could not be real at all.

"And they were very curious indeed when I couldn't tell them where you were, where they could find you. I thought the best way out was the truth, I said we'd had a fight."

"Am I to assume the police are now hunting me with sirens baying?"

"No, you're to notify them, call when you get back here— Maeve, where are you? This won't do at all."

"I'm perfectly safe and well, at a pub, and you know as well as I do that after last night I must come to grips with this thing, it can't go on a moment longer—" She almost added, If it's not already too late, perhaps I won't be back, I don't want, now or ever, to bore you.

This time a silence from him. "Skipping a lot of things we're going to have to say to each other, to fill up the big gap in between," he said, "you happen to be my world and pretty well my life in this short time whether you know it or not. Will you for Christ's sake be careful of yourself?"

"Yes, I promise." Don't say good-bye, again. A word that threw long shadows. She wanted to say, I love you, Fen, and didn't, and was sorry about it instantly. She thought how awful it would be if anything happened to her—a car she hadn't seen in time—she wouldn't ever be able to tell him, I love you, I love you.

She wiped tears from her cheeks after she had hung up, the first she had shed since the bunch of violets had struck his sleeping face.

It never occurred to her that there might be any danger in seeking Desmond.

When she got back to her place at the end of the banquette, she saw something that froze her gaze. On top of the upright piano was a half-full pint mug of beer, a pair of dark glasses cocked over the mug, its earpieces thrust through the handle. A visual signature of Desmond's. Left at his place, in any pub, when he went to talk to someone, or to get himself a plate of food.

On cue, the plump dark-haired young man who had been playing the piano on her first visit there came back from the bar with a steaming plate, sat down on the piano stool facing away from the keyboard and toward her, put his plate on the table in front of her, and began hungrily to eat.

Another man had come in and sat down on the banquette when she had been on the telephone. Red-haired, blue-eyed; the Spread Eagle had a strong Irish flavor indeed. He was deep in a tabloid. A spread devoted to the Gaymere kidnapping. "Family Waits Release Terms for Missing Money Baron and His Beautiful Wife." Pictures, Lois on horseback, the O.B.E. being conferred on an unsmiling Edwin, peacocks in the rose garden at Hildegrave House.

She turned to the dark man. Very directly, she said, "Good morning. You do play a lovely piano. I heard you the other night, an old favorite of mine, so few people know it . . . 'The Young May Moon.' "

"Oh, a lovely song," he said. "I played it by request as a matter of fact."

Her eyes went to the beer mug above and behind his head with the sunglasses fastened into its handle.

"Queer coincidence, a friend of mine wears *his* glasses on his glass, and it's one of *his* favorite songs—"

Impossible, but it happened. He laughed in a friendly way, reached for the mug, removed the glasses, took a deep draught, and said, "Could be the same fellow. I got this habit from him. You wouldn't be talking about Desmond Byrne?"

"Yes, I am." Calm and cool. She felt the blue eyes, to her left, briefly on her; then he returned to his paper.

"Sure, he was the one that asked for that song. He had to hum a couple of bars of it for me before I picked it up. And then what did he do but leave before I was well into it, the ungrateful fellow, but you know Desmond, restless—out the door with him and that was that. I haven't seen him since."

"Have you any idea where I can reach him? It's about something that's actually rather important to me, and to him."

She was reminded by her own words of the classified ads that said if someone would get in touch with someone else they would learn something to their advantage.

Reaching again for his glass, Jimmy Doolan's cuff caught his half-finished plate of shepherd's pie and sent it tumbling to the carpet.

"Oh, hell," he wailed.

The red-haired man looked up, looked over, smiled a little at the small accident, studied Maeve again for a moment with a polite male tribute of interest: her curry-colored silk jersey tunic, dark red-chestnut hair falling soft and shining from the center parting over the high wide white forehead, the long slim hand, fingers through the handle of a nearly full mug. Then he resumed the Gaymeres, whose story went on to the next page, and the next.

At his sympathetic smile over the tumbling food, she had noted without thinking about it that he had two front teeth missing, one top, one bottom.

An elderly man came over with a dustpan to clean up the food and broken crockery. Jimmy Doolan had gone back for another plate. When he seated himself, a white-haired woman with a cane hobbled over and shouted a request in his ear.

Not wanting to look overeager, in a hurry, Maeve waited while he played "The Rose of Tralee" and "Greensleeves."

She occupied herself in the meantime with an unlovely vision of the police, who would have been busy now if they had gotten a picture of her. Showing it to men she imagined they would usually keep an eye on, who heard things and were willing to tell them for a little money, men with stained hats and soiled teeth, in obscure pubs or dusty beer-scented flats. "Do you know this woman? Do you know of a Maeve Vaughan, born Devlin, U.S. citizen but spends a lot of time in Ireland?" Fenway Vaughan's new wife.

Fen had a picture of her; she knew he had. A snapshot, black and white, hair flying in the wind, a half-smile at something she couldn't now remember. He kept it in his billfold. "Not for other people to see. But just to refresh my memory when I have to be away from you for an hour or so."

He hadn't given it to them. But then, he couldn't seriously think—

Jimmy Doolan spun around on his piano stool. The red-haired man came back with another pint and Doolan waited for the console to respond to its meal of coins, and put his face close to Maeve's.

"Desmond's a private kind of fellow but as you're a friend—" He looked at her with pleasure. Desmond's kind of girl; style and class. "There's a lass, works for him in some kind of charitable organization he takes an interest in, sermons on the street for peace and unity—" He was tempted to wink but thought that it wouldn't quite do. "She was in here with him, one night, and stopped to talk to me on the way back from the ladies', as we have a cousin in common. I asked her where she lived, thinking I might see a bit more of her. She might and might not know how you could get in touch with Desmond, or where he lives. I'll give you her address if you have a bit of paper—"

The address was 14 Mote Street. The street was, he said, a bit north and east of St. George's Square, cross over Lupus Street and continue, a short walk, she couldn't miss it. And yes, thank you very much, he would enjoy a pint.

The man on her left turned to her and said in a soft polite voice, "I don't know would you like this newspaper, ma'am. I'm finished with it."

"Thank you, there's something I glanced at that I'd like to take a better look at."

She turned back to the Gaymere story and found the photograph of Fen to comfort herself with. "Mrs. Gaymere's brother, Mr. Fenway Vaughan, a director of the New York publishing house of Fenway & Vaughan, says he last saw his sister the morning after the explosion of the car bomb at Gaymere House and . . ."

His eyes, his forehead, his hairline; the hint of humor and sweetness about the fine composed mouth.

Fen, darling, I wish you were right here, right now.

Underneath his picture and its caption was a photograph of a boy astride a bicycle. "The unseen witness. Details on page eight."

She didn't take time to read it. There were things to be done. She looked at Fen's face for a moment more; and then she got up and left the Spread Eagle.

FOUR

Lois, where are you?

And Maeve . . . where are *you?*

He reluctantly forced himself back to *The Times*. "New disclosure on the apparent kidnapping of Edwin Gaymere . . ."

He had angrily agreed to himself that she probably had reason to flee the house. He couldn't remember exactly what he had said to her, wakened by the soft blow in the face, but he was aware that he had wanted to strike out, strike back, savagely.

He had been dreaming, and it was still vividly with him, about something awful happening to Lois, and in his dream Maeve's face kept changing place with Lois's and there intruded in turn the long lazily stretching body of Desmond Byrne on the hearthrug, passionately holding Maeve or was it Lois, and then a cry, a shriek, blood, and a thud of violets against his cheek—

What had she, in turn, said to him? Nothing, in her defense. Not a word. ". . . draw the scent away from you, at least one small thing you won't have to worry and wonder about . . ."

Maeve, I need you, badly.

Warm against him, graceful and yielding, but with a certain toughness and spirit under the soft pliability that he liked and admired. You couldn't, he supposed, have it both ways, have her accepting the lash with bent and willing back.

Her natural gaiety, her way of being amused and amusing without working at it . . . and the other, shadowed side of her nature, the streak of sadness, aloneness, which he hoped in time to be able to banish. "I am a product of aunts." Way back there, years away, in a Park Avenue apartment filled with noisy strangers, and then the one person in the room he had, somehow, always known. Who was now at the very center of his life.

"New disclosure . . ."

A witness turned up by the police, he read, wearily focusing his attention on the newsprint. A boy of seventeen, son of the cook, Mrs. Grady, at Hildegrave House. He was bicycling back from the village of Hildegrave and was just approaching a crossroads where the main road was met at right angles by a steeply descending lane between high grassy banks and over-hanging trees.

He heard a sound that had startled him a little at the time, a man whistling a tune, high above his head. "I thought God in heaven was whistling to me," he said, grinning, to the police. Then he heard the engine of an approaching car, from beyond the top of the bank. He saw a man come out of the long grass under a tree, carrying a yellow-painted road barrier which he set up across the mouth of the lane. What kind of man, how had he been dressed? Oh, just a man, dark hair, a roadman, working clothes . . .

He bicycled on. He heard, from behind him, a sharp single ringing crack. "No, sir, I didn't think anything about it at the time, I knew it was gunfire but I thought someone was out after rooks or rabbits, as they often are about here. . . ."

His interrogator was a very sharp young sergeant who happened to be taking piano lessons because his girl loved to listen to him picking out a tune in her mother's parlor.

Would he happen to remember what the signal tune, whistled in the treetops, was?

Yes, funny thing, it was a favorite of his mother's. It was called "The Young May Moon."

"He won't thank you for that, snatching away his favorite

love song and handing it to the police on a silver platter—whatever made you pick that one?"

Impatiently, "I don't know, what does a song matter anyway, it sticks in your head, I heard him whistling it a few nights ago, this modern-day truck has no tune to it, but that's a tune. . . ."

Tom Gaymere, over the telephone, spoke with an unnatural calm.

"Things are working out well, Fen, very well."

"Are you drugged, or drunk, or something, Tom? You sound—"

"I am just moving along *very* quietly from minute to minute, Fen, or I'll explode and splash back off the walls. I've just gotten my instructions. I won't endanger you by telling you what they are—"

"Endanger, hell, I won't go to the door and shout it down the mews, I've got to know."

"Well, then, I'm to fly to Dublin, the first plane I can get. Hire a car at the airport, drive it into the city, and go to a parking garage under construction on a street near Merrion Square. I'm to drive into the lower level, which has been completed and is ready for use. There will be a lot of men on the site, I'm told—they can't, I suppose, *all* be involved in kidnap—and of course I'm to come alone. I am to leave the car at the first, upward turn of the entrance ramp, inside the building, and leave my attaché case on the front seat, with the money. Then I'm to walk to the Shelbourne Hotel on Stephen's Green and hail a cab there and go back to the airport. I'm to take the first plane to London, and if I am seen to make a call, or behave in any way out of the ordinary, they will be killed."

"Do the police know about this?"

"Yes. I've just talked to them. They told me to go ahead."

A parking garage under construction . . .

Fen could see the bustle and confusion, the stacked metals, the tarpaulins, the shouting men, the towering cranes, the cement trucks, the steady roar of noise pierced by the clanging and clanking, the protection of shielded and mysterious heights, some of them frightfully dangerous except to the men who knew every girder, every safe way down. A good place, if the police sent unseen men with or after Tom Gaymere, for an effective armed resistance and even for a lightning escape down some ringing warren.

But then the police probably would not, could not, act until Edwin and Lois were released. Or Interpol, or whoever was taking over at the Dublin end. He had no special illusions about the importance of Lois's life to Her Majesty's government; but he thought that Edwin's continued existence might be considered to be very important indeed.

"They said—sorry, *he* said, not the nice soft voice but another one, Irish too, nasal, tough—that on receipt of the money Mrs. Gaymere will be freed and should be home safely by, at the latest, tomorrow morning. He said that it was realized that the arrangement about the political prisoners, for Edwin, would consume more time and that they would continue to hold him patiently. *'Patiently!'* " Tom repeated in a high voice beginning to be edged with hysteria.

"Had he any proof to offer about either of them?"

"A tape from Edwin, this time, very much like Lois's, which I listened to over the phone. He's well, he's not allowed to see her, she's in a room nearby, and he adds, 'Tell Balt for Christ's sake not to drag his heels, I have work to do and I want to get on with it.' Just as if he were sitting at the head of his own conference table at Gaymere House—"

"Were the police monitoring the call, do you know?"

"Yes. All they told me was that it came in from Ireland."

"Did he say *how* Lois would get home?"

"No, just that she will be freed. They'd never be fools enough to deliver her. With Edwin still in their hands, she might come straight to you, not want to face the police and all the questioning and confusion by herself, will you be there?"

"Yes," Fen said grimly. "Yes, I'll be here."

"Give my love to Maeve and tell her not to worry, everything's going to be all right."

"I'll do that, Tom. Good luck."

The restorers and developers turning blocks of Pimlico into charming and newly expensive dwellings had not yet caught up with Mote Street.

Paint was peeling, plaster was cracking, on the once cream-colored houses with their double-pillared porches. At Number 14, the ground-floor tenant had settled on yellowed sheets tacked unevenly behind the glass as his window treatment. On the broken pavement beside the porch was a small dead cedar tree in a pot, a bony geranium, arthritic-looking in its joints, and a dusty thin-ribbed yellow cat.

She had found the street, which apparently extended only one block, and diagonally at that, after taking a few wrong turnings. The red-haired man, who had left the Spread Eagle right on her heels, came up to her and said, "I'm heading for a place not far from Mote Street. Will I take you there, if you don't know the neighborhood?"

The streets of Pimlico, she had noticed before, were extremely quiet; now, on Sunday, they seemed deserted.

He looked friendly, harmless; it was perhaps New York-inspired caution that made her say with a smile, "Thank you, no. I have errands on the way there, things I want to pick up, I won't detain you."

She walked very fast toward St. George's Square and thought she heard footsteps behind her, his. Politely, to illustrate her errand, she stopped at a little store on Lupus Street and bought at random two fresh pears and emerged again.

Before she pressed the greened brass button next to the slip bearing two names, Jane Conroy and Ellen Coyle, she took one last look down the street. A bicyclist turned the corner: the red-haired man. He raised his hand in a cheerful salute. "You found her, that's good." Her? Then he must have been listening to what she and Doolan had been saying to each other. And why not? A man alone, with only his newspaper for company, in a pub.

There was an indecisive buzzing from the door-release mechanism, as though the person buzzing was not at all sure she wanted a caller. A light pressure, a second, a third; Maeve just managed to turn the knob before the last, uncertain buzz from above flickered off.

No attempt at an entrance hall; just a steep stairway going up, lit by a wall bracket holding a bare bulb of what must be the minimum available wattage. A timid, young face showed in the crack of the barely opened door to the right of the landing. The white paint of the door was smeared and dirty and there were scuff marks near the bottom of it as though some previous tenant ordinarily gained admittance by kicking at it.

Even in the dim light, Maeve recognized the wan features of the girl who had handed around the paper cups of tea at the

Blessed Union rally at Marble Arch. She had obviously been crying.

Briskly and pleasantly, Maeve identified herself. "May I come in for a moment? I'm looking for the address of a friend and I thought you might be able to help me. Jimmy Doolan directed me to you."

How like a conspirator I sound, she thought.

"Yes, come in, but if it's Ellen you want she's out—"

The shabby little room was clean and neat. Jane Conroy looked at her elegant silk-suited visitor as if she found her presence in some way reassuring.

"But first, what's wrong, can I do anything . . . ?"

The tears came again. "The police have just been here," the girl said, wiping her cheek with the back of her hand. "He was kind, he was Irish, a man named Riordan—he told me the men who work for the Union, some of them, have criminal records—and that it may not be all honest and aboveboard—I suppose it will be in all the papers—I don't know how I'll ever face my mother, and my uncle's the priest—"

"What did the police want of you? Surely they don't suspect you of anything?"

"Information on anyone in the Union I know, their names, where they live, exactly what they do for the Union, day and night—he had a noteboook, taking it all down. When I think of our prayers, and our masses, and our novenas, and our meetings—and then, they wanted to know about Mr. Byrne . . ."

Her voice trailed off and a light came over her face. Maeve recognized it: adoration. The great god Desmond.

She felt a wrench of pity for the earnest, dedicated, used young woman.

"His is the address I want, as a matter of fact—and were you able to tell them anything they didn't know?"

"Just that he's a writer, and he gave, very generously, of his time, and did our booklets and things for us, and sometimes wrote a grand kind of letter that could be sent to very rich people asking for donations, contributions."

"I'm a very old friend of his," Maeve said, beginning to tire of the idea of Desmond as an old friend. "Tell me where I can find him, do. In return I advise you and Ellen to go home, right away, and then if any little storm breaks it won't be over your heads." She hesitated and then asked delicately, "How are your funds, or have you given them all away? If, as I really think you should, you decide to go home today, or tomorrow at the latest?"

The girl flushed. "A pound or so. Ellen has a bit—"

Maeve took out thirty of her thirty-five pounds. "Take this as an indefinite loan, I'll give you my address in Dublin. It will get the two of you on the boat, at least. I know Mr. Byrne would want you safely away in case there's going to be any trouble, I'm more or less acting on his behalf. Now, where did you say he lived?"

She could see that Jane Conroy was already mentally packing and fleeing, and facing her mother and her uncle the priest; and that she was soothed at this prospect by the suggestion that Mr. Byrne, golden Mr. Byrne, the writer, was taking care of her vicariously.

"I had to deliver a package to him there, once. Caudle Street, near Lambeth Palace, I don't remember the number but there's a dressmaker in the building where his flat is, he's right at the top of the first flight of stairs—I don't like to take that money, Mrs. Vaughan—"

"Mr. Byrne," Maeve said firmly, "would absolutely insist that you did. The last thing in the world he would want is trouble for innocent people."

FIVE

The silver pants suit glowed coldly in the dressmaker's window at the street level of the house in Caudle Street.

Maeve watched her taxi hurry down the street and turn a corner, and she stood alone in the Sunday silence, in front of the green door to the side of the window. His flat, Jane Conroy had said, was at the top of the first flight of stairs; she hadn't said whether it was front or back. But she thought she felt him, looking down at her, from behind stilled folds of white.

Nonsense; nine chances out of ten, he probably wouldn't be there, anyway, the elusive Desmond.

The green door was unlocked. She went in and for a moment leaned, braced her back against it, and drew a long breath. She felt herself driven, and alone, and not at all confident about her errand.

Summon up Fen, have his company as you go up the stairs. An arm about her, warm and strong. A palm against hers, dry, caressing, electric. She almost heard the faint rustle of cloth as he moved swiftly to embrace her, almost saw the near gleam of taut skin over a finely angled cheekbone, the flecks in the eyes; up close, they would be the darkest blue in this dully lighted hall. Mentally, she touched and smoothed, as she often did, a particularly vigorous dark eyebrow hair that corkscrewed down and threatened to entangle itself with his eyelashes.

His voice, beside a sunny window in a blue and white bedroom a remote distance away: "Are you quite safe in threatening him with whatever you know?"

"Yes. I think so."

Yes, I think so . . . Michael Bye, 2A, the brass-framed tenant list said. He might not answer a buzz, if he was there, but he would know her knock. She went up the stairs, saw that 2A was the front apartment, paused a second or two before the door, and then struck it lightly, three times, with the knuckles of her first two fingers.

The door was opened, not with any caution, but hospitably and wide. Desmond stood in the doorway, smiling down at her.

"What a clever girl you are, to have found me. Come in, Maeve." He made a welcoming gesture with a backward sweep of his arm.

She moved past him, graceful, erect, outwardly relaxed. A raging frontal attack wouldn't work; there was nothing to stop him instantly and firmly ejecting her if he met with open hostility on his doorstep.

Her manner was neither friendly nor unfriendly; but civil and cool.

"Attractive place you have here, Desmond, much nicer than one would think from the looks of Caudle Street."

It was a very large bed-sitting room and he must have furnished it himself. She assumed Caudle Street landlords did not supply Persian prayer rugs on a shining floor stained burgundy, a Napoleonic sleigh bed, a great sofa and two deep chairs covered in soft brandy-brown leather, a wall of books in glittering chrome steel shelves, a round dining table in rosy faded mahogany, Queen Anne chairs for the diners.

From some concealed speaker, the BBC provided Beethoven's Ninth Symphony.

She paused in her deliberate, casual survey of the room.

"Yes, very nice."

"You know me," Desmond said. "I like a little comfort, wherever I am."

Although she knew he was a good actor, she sensed that he

was not surprised by her appearance; not only not surprised, but obscurely, and almost amusedly, pleased.

Perhaps Jane Conroy, with second thoughts about giving his whereabouts, had warned him by telephone that he was about to have a visitor. A Mrs. Vaughan. Or—the red-haired man. He might be someone, of Desmond's.

She turned and saw him adjusting a rather complicated-looking door lock.

"Now, will you have a drink, Maeve?"

"No, thank you."

"I'll help myself, then, and while I pour you can tell me how you found me." Pleasant, amiable; ridiculous to think of the words as somehow threatening.

She sat down in one of the leather chairs. "I have been a victim, for some reason we're about to go into, of fruit and flowers and music—of what was known in our grandmothers' day as unwelcome attentions. It was 'The Young May Moon' that found you for me, I won't bore you with the laborious plodding in between."

His back was to her and she thought she saw it stiffen a little.

Then he turned and lifted his drink to her. "Well, your health, love. One way or another, I'm lucky you're here."

She looked at him as thoroughly as she had ever done in her life.

Michael Bye in weekend clothing, price no object. Trousers of palest velvety fawn corduroy, tailored to the lean waist and long supple legs. A shirt of thin crisp cream silk, sleeves rolled negligently to the forearms. The chestnut-colored tie he had worn on the hearthrug.

A tall building across the street kept sun from the room; lamps were on and warmed the shining gold of his hair, found no bottom at all to the large, beautiful azure eyes. The sun had gotten at his skin, gilded it and decked it with the soft informal freckles which made an amused comment on the magnificent bone structure beneath. A force, a purpose, a magnetism came from him as always, sharp as the best cologne on the shadowy air of his room.

Pleased at her presence, yes, for some reason. But wary and watchful, cat-braced.

He went to the telephone on a bamboo table beside her chair and dialed a number and said, above her head, "Hello there— Desmond Byrne, hereafter known as the other man. Your wife's here, I wouldn't want you worrying about what she's gotten herself into. We're about to embark on a sociable afternoon. It's been a devil of a long time since we've had a chance to be alone together. Would you like to speak to her?''

She was very much puzzled. Her tendrils were out, feeling the air. Why had he called Fen? Another bunch of violets or basket of fruit, to further confuse and divide them?

Let him know, somehow, it wasn't as casual and comfortable, this visit, as Desmond had made it sound.

"Hello, Fenway," she said.

A second of silence; but she heard and felt his response. Then he said, "Hello, Maeve. Is everything all right?"

"Everything's going to be fine. And at your end?"

"I assume he's there beside you—yes, all right, I hope."

"Desmond and I are about to discuss—as I went over, with you—what the plot of this particular book is, I don't imagine it will take very long, I'll be home soon."

"Where are you?"

Desmond's ear had been bent lovingly close to her head. He took the receiver from her hand, said into it, "She's quite safe in my arms, Vaughan," and quietly replaced it.

Maeve stared at him. Then she said, "Oh. Are you taping this? Something else for your plot?"

"Plot, is it," he said. *"Plot?"*

"Yes, plot." She was infuriated at the way he had terminated her contact with Fen; but show him any weakness, fury, or pain, and he would leap on it.

"You're using me for something, I haven't figured out what. This Michael Bye novel, Desmond—what's it about? Why are you pursuing a woman who is married to and very much in love with another man, what can you possibly hope to gain by it?"

"You, darling."

More material for his tape? She would give him something to decorate the tape.

Not liking his standing over her, she got up and went to the window and leaned against the sill.

"If this doesn't stop, all of it, immediately, I will take you and your Blessed Union and turn it inside out. I won't just mumble the information to any passer-by. I have a friend in the news department at CBS. It would make a marvelous, juicy story, and of course you're frightfully photogenic, which helps—"

The telephone rang. Fen? Not a hope.

Desmond listened. ". . . yes, well, Elissa darling, perhaps later, perhaps not, I may be otherwise occupied this evening." He turned back to Maeve. "Do go on. I wouldn't want to miss any of this."

"I don't know if you remember, one morning about four, several years ago, telling me all about it, and how your disinterested attempts to aid your mother country might make you rich. I don't know who all your little helpers are but I know that foul Cooley and I could guess at some of the other names, I have a good memory for names, especially when they're people I dislike, despise."

He gave her a long, thoughtful look, drained his drink, and poured another one.

"Whatever publicity you get ought to be enough to stop the money rolling in. And of course the police are already interested."

He walked over to her.

"You're rather a daring young woman, Maeve, aren't you? . . . As a matter of fact, I always liked that quality of yours. What makes you think you can come here alone, and threaten me?"

He seemed calm; he smiled, but there was a whiteness around his mouth. "For your information, the people in back and above us are away for the weekend. The shop downstairs of course is closed. You've no doubt spotted what a quiet street this is. . . . I'm glad you reminded me that you had been told all about the Union. To tell you the truth that little conversation with you had slipped my mind."

Don't show him fright; although she was beginning to know her first fear, with him.

"Come off it, Desmond. I'm known to be with you, you took care of that."

"With me, yes—but nobody, most especially and particularly your husband, knows where."

"Agreed, then?" she asked coolly. "You'll drop your wooing and leave me alone?"

The Ninth Symphony suddenly halted.

A man's crisp voice said, "We interrupt this program to

bring you a special news bulletin. Edwin Gaymere has escaped his kidnappers and is free, in Dublin. He was thought to have been abducted by the revolutionary arm of the I.R.A., which has been repeatedly denied. He had been held in a house on Merrion Square, owned by a Mrs. Thomas Delanoy. He told police that he had overheard plans for his own murder at the hands of the men who were holding him. A city-wide search for the kidnappers is on. Mrs. Delanoy's housekeeper, Mrs. Ellen Locket, has been taken into custody. Lois Gaymere, who had been reported as being with her husband, is not in the house and there is no information yet on her whereabouts. We will give you more on the Gaymere escape as the details come in."

The first, terrible thought that dropped into the stunned vacuum of her mind was, Fen is hearing this. Fen just heard this.

A house on Merrion Square. Brenda's house.

And she herself, off for an afternoon with Desmond. As he had announced to Fen, safe in his arms.

It was the Byrne temper that, for the moment, undid him.

"Jesus Christ, the fools, the bloody blundering damned *fools* . . . !"

He flung his half-filled glass at the bookshelves and the smashing sounds met Beethoven, richly resuming.

Then he turned, his eyes on Maeve, and both of them listened to the resounding silence that lay beneath the music.

She felt as if she were looking at him as through a telescope. Enraged, alone, far away, but brought near and clear by the lens. A beautiful golden child whose toy had been seized from him, or broken.

"Heavens, Desmond," she said, and was surprised by the hollow quiet sound of her own voice, "all smashed, is it? Smashed to smithereens . . ."

The telescope showed him moving toward her, a slow, contained walk. Coming to a few inches away from her. And then, carefully, putting his arms around her and resting his cheek on her hair.

"I forgot I can't say anything and everything in front of you, always." The voice from far away too, very low.

She felt totally unable to move.

The stone had been tossed into the pond, but the ripples hadn't started; the surface lay still.

"You didn't hear that, love," he said tenderly. "It wouldn't do at all, for you to have heard that. Not after—"

One little ripple started, where the stone had dropped into the pond.

Not after all our years together.

There are things you cannot be allowed to know about people. Even if you have been very close, very long.

She wasn't entirely sure, yet, what it was about him that she knew.

SIX

Physically speaking, Edwin Gaymere had been quite comfortable in Maeve Devlin Vaughan's apartment, on the fourth floor of her Aunt Brenda's house.

Patching together the moments of consciousness on the way that had brought him there, in between those intervals when he was no doubt under heavy sedation, he remembered the clamping hands, the blow, after Trann had been shot, killed, in the innocent green lane with the tree shadows playing softly on the yellow road barrier.

More darkness, feet and hands tied, an elastic bandage over his mouth, something vaguely familiar to his eye—an interior wall, heavy sweating blocks of gray stone, a great oil-smelling lawn roller, rakes and hoes leaning against the wall . . . the garden hut at the west, rear entrance to Hildegrave House. There hadn't been a head gardener for a year, no amount of money would buy staff these days, and Trann had arranged to have a man and his son in from the village thirty hours a week to tend the lawns and gardens close to the house, and let the rest go to meadow and wild flowers. . . .

A voice that seemed to come from a distance: "Food, no, he'll hold until tomorrow morning, I believe these fellows, these money fellows, are well fed, caviar I'm told is very sustaining. . . ." An Irish voice, dark, hard, resentful.

Some time later, helicopter rotors whirring, thumping over his head, a starry black sky through the window; he was not sitting up but flat on his back and his muscles howled, screamed with pain.

He lifted his head joltingly, felt a sharp prick in his arm. More darkness.

The motion of an automobile, the swish of a great door opening, the ascent in a small elevator; three men in it made a crowd. He was blindfolded but he knew there were two of them besides him.

They must have untied him while he had slept, in the big, high, comfortable bed. He woke without pain. There was no way to tell whether it was night or day; he saw, through the thin crisp stuff of the long, ruffled white window curtains, the panes and the padlocked shutters beyond. The bedside lamp shone on a man of perhaps thirty, sitting watching him; thin, fair, featureless, except for small sharp blue eyes. A pistol, German from the looks of it, large in his loosely clasping thin hand.

"Rules of the game as follows," the man said, Irish voice but not the dark harsh one. "Your wife is in the next room. We won't rope and tie you now, but if you make any noise, not that you'd be heard, this house is solid as a rock and all closed up until Her Grace, whoever she may be, returns—if you do, your wife will be shot immediately."

There was a knock at the bedroom door. The man unlocked it and took a tray from the floor outside, relocked the door, and served him. Tea and toast, the Irish soda bread pale brown, sweet crisp.

"You won't need your clothes today, she's got a robe hanging on the bathroom hook ought to fit you."

She.

Lois bought the same kind of robe, in Paris, by the half dozen.

When, later, wrapped in voluminous white terry cloth to his ankles, he prowled the room under his guard's gaze, he was able without any trouble at all to identify the legal occupant of this room. Maeve Elizabeth Devlin, said a bookplate in a handsomely bound *David Copperfield*.

Trann, at breakfast—"One in the bosom of your family, sir"—giggling about it.

After the first white flare of astonishment, he wasted little time in wondering how and where she came into it; he was not given to the practice of wondering. Lois had said he'd only known her, Fen had, a very short time before he married her.

He maintained his surface composure; the wrath inside, the outraged knowledge of being stripped for the time being of power, was doing unpleasant things to the rhythm of his heart.

Well, a matter of business after all. Whatever these people wanted would of course be given to them by *his* people, forthwith, and it would be over, a damned nuisance, the whole thing, but it would be over.

The thought of the headlines, the radio and television news bulletins, calmed him a little. A silver lining, perhaps. A sort of fringe benefit, in its way.

It must be day; because at the proper lapse of time after breakfast, lunch was served; and then, after endless hours, dinner. He thought he heard a woman's murmur outside the door when the trays arrived. Not Maeve Vaughan; a brogue. He occupied himself with letters that could not now, unfortunately, be dictated to Trann; and he read, at intervals, Maeve's copy of *The Decline and Fall of the Roman Empire*.

They must be drugging his food; when he half-woke, at some time which must have been night, real night, he heard the changing of the guard, the big thin dark man taking over. He sounded remote, like a distant and barely audible radio impossibly high above the bed—no doubt the drugs did this—and his syllables limped and clung together as if he was under the influence of drink.

". . . touched me on the shoulder and wanted to know if it was my car illegally parked across the street. Christ, I almost fell at his feet in a faint. I'll be glad when it's down the well with this one . . . by this time tomorrow we'll be out of it. . . ."

The other man made a hissing, silencing noise.

Edwin Gaymere got the message, blurred and limping as it was. This, then, wasn't an ordinary business matter, which one would wait out and walk away from, back into everyday life. He was to be put down a well. Alive, dead? It didn't matter in the long run.

A cold little answer to a cold little question in his head: why had no one thought to conceal the identity of the apartment's occupant? It would have seemed an elementary precaution. Particularly when she was related to him by marriage; an awkward business to say the least. The puzzle now resolved itself. It didn't matter at all; because he would not be alive to discuss being incarcerated in Maeve Vaughan's flat.

He was not good at physical adventuring. There was only one answer now, the immediate and powerful voice of money. Not the dark man, he wasn't sober enough to grasp an offer, and he looked rough, vindictive. But the fair one . . . more pliable.

Sketch for him certain capture, marked bills, prison, or a hunted life on the run, disaster around every corner, informers whispering to the rustle of pound notes, the end of freedom and manhood, the virtual end of life.

Over his morning toast and tea, he delivered his midnight analysis, very coldly and eloquently, to the fair man and watched with a match-flicker of hope the picture of his future, studied, sinking in, striking at brain and emotion.

"There's another solution for you . . ."

He paused to sip tea; his throat was dry.

"I will establish a bank account in any name you give me—preferably with no criminal record attached to it—and I will pay into it five thousand pounds a year for ten years." His banker's instincts told him the value of security, continuity.

"How do I know you won't rat on me?"

"How can I? I don't know your name and I don't want to know it. Your description would fit thousands of young men. As far as I am concerned, my other captor, besides that dark chap, had gray hair and was in his fifties, and limped."

He saw the fair man mentally studying his ten-year bank account. Not a fantastic sum, unswallowable; but a prudent and mildly generous payment for the continued existence of Edwin Gaymere.

He went quickly on, "Nothing to it, leave me, and leave the doors unlocked, but first get that woman, whoever she is, out of the house for an hour or so. If I were you, I'd temporarily lose myself, in London, say, they'll have your cohorts and whoever is running this operation safely in prison in no time."

His wallet had been untouched; he took from a concealed inner pocket the five-hundred-pound note he always carried for emergencies. "This will take care of your expenses until you can start drawing on your account. Go over to the writing desk and put down your new name. If I were you, I'd make it a common one, as a matter of fact I'd go find a telephone directory and see which name has the longest listings and choose that one. . . ."

It was the chairman of the board speaking, with the unquestioned authority of millions upon millions of pounds sterling in his voice. Even discussing money gave him back himself; he felt confident and at ease.

"By the way, is my wife here or isn't she?"

"No, I think she's in England somewhere, I don't think they planned to harm *her*—" There was an eager capitulation in the fair man's eyes. Almost to himself, he added, as though in apology to an unseen person, "Not to put too fine a point upon it, I never did much like the idea of killing, anyway—"

"Who is 'they'?"

"That's not a part of this," the man said sharply. "I'll go into the other room and get the directory." He looked at the treasury note in a denomination he had never seen before and thrust it lovingly into his pocket.

SEVEN

Feeling as though he had been shot in the stomach, Fen sat staring at the radio.

Mrs. Thomas Delanoy's house . . . Brenda, her pearls and soft voice and scent of roses, as she sat in his living room in New York, talking to his father. . . . "But Gaymere is asking on bended knee for a bomb or a bullet."

Or a vengeful political kidnapping.

The signal tune that would release a bullet into Trann's brain, whistled from a treetop in a Surrey Lane, "The Young May Moon."

The notes of it seemed to drift in from the mews, on the gently moving air. Whistled in the night, while Maeve lay tensed and braced beside him. The champagne, "To us, forever, love darling, D."

"She's quite safe in my arms."

Lois had not been with Edwin. Where, right now, was Lois, what was happening to her, particularly when the news was out that he had escaped, kicked over the applecart? "He told

police that he had overheard plans for his own murder. . . ."
Was Lois's death part of their plan too?

His head ached badly. He found himself, after the long strain, the waiting and worrying, and now the thudding burning questions, hardly able to think.

"Hello, Fenway." She never used his full name. Was it, as he had thought, a statement of her purpose and innocence in seeking out Desmond, a correction, which Desmond wouldn't be able to spot, of his insinuations about the nature of her visit?

Or was it, in this terrible new glare of knowledge, some kind of thrusting aside of her husband, some veiled announcement of flight, separation, that he had totally failed to grasp.

How competent she had been, lying to the police about Desmond and the Blessed Union, how thoroughly believable she had sounded.

The notice on the front door, To this case I have given £100. Cooley, awful Cooley. "She was pleased enough to drink down the scotch I bought her. . . ."

Could there be some passion of patriotism for Ireland she had kept in serene concealment from him, which would lead her into a scheme to still Edwin's harsh attacking Establishment voice?

By the way, Mr. Vaughan, we'd appreciate a photograph of your wife.

Only one thing to do, with Lois looking him in the face. Inform and betray. Call the police. "I'm not sure how my wife comes into this, but she's with a man who could very well be involved—I'll tell you exactly why. And there's the matter of the use of her aunt's house—"

Turn on the police, turn them out, sirens shouting, after Maeve. His lovely Maeve. "Madame, you are under arrest—"

You say you have no idea where your wife is?

No, there's nothing I can suggest outside a flat-by-flat search of the city of London. Oh, and don't forget the hotels. And then there's always Greenwich, and Richmond, and Kew . . .

He could hear the radioed description, the sound of it tangling with traffic noises, ". . . five feet seven and a half inches tall, dark red or auburn hair, green eyes, age about thirty, identifying mark small scar near right elbow, last seen wearing . . ." Wearing what? He had no idea what clothing she had taken when he scalded her out, alone, into the night.

There was something wrong with his face, uncomfortable.

He brushed the back of his hand against it and felt the cold untidy tears.

He walked once, twice, three times the length of the room. Mac sensed his pain and trouble and paced beside him, looking up into his face.

Of course, she was innocent, but Desmond might know something that could save Lois, and Desmond had to be found, and she was with him. . . . There had to be some rational explanation for the use of the house on Merrion Square. Desmond, often in Dublin, would know Brenda was away, know the house was occupied only by—what was her name?—Mrs. Locket—

He deliberately closed his mind, made it blank, and went to the telephone. Ask for Detective-Sergeant Vesey—

The ringing of the telephone bell confused him for a second; why should the phone be ringing here when its next intended ring was to be at New Scotland Yard? He picked up the receiver.

"Fen?" Voice a little blurred and sleepy sounding. "It's me . . . Lois. I'm all right, I've been let go, it's the weirdest thing . . ."

Feeling as though his legs would not support him, he sat down suddenly on the arm of the apricot sofa.

"Lois, thank God—where are you?"

"You sound awful, Fen, raw—I woke up, or came to, a while back. I was sitting on a grass bank at the side of the road, up against what must be the longest fence of rhododendrons in England, all in blossom. . . . I got up, staggering a bit, three cars went by, I suppose they thought I was drunk, and then a nice man stopped for me, I said I wanted a phone booth, I didn't tell him who I was because I can't face the police just now, I'll soon be on my way to you, and then I will allow myself to scream and sob the house down. Right now, I suppose I'm still full of some calming stuff—in any case, he let me out in the center of a little town named Tibbettbury, and that's where I'm calling from. I'm going to hire a car and a driver, there's a place next door, except right now they're all tied up with somebody's funeral, so I'll just drink tea for a while and maybe have some whiskey when I get my mind back. If the car hire man is right, I should be there no later than eight. I don't know where they've put Edwin, have you heard from him . . . ?"

"He's all right. He's in Dublin. Free."

Tom's money delivery, he thought with the part of his mind that was still functioning, must have gone smoothly and swiftly; whoever had been holding Lois—it appeared now that she had probably been in England all the time—must have released her immediately upon notification. They would, he supposed, have drugged and blindfolded her, put her in a car or a van, waited until the long country road was empty, quickly propped their soft unconscious bundle on the grassy bank, and then driven off.

Everything, almost everything, all right, then. He rubbed his eyes. Edwin free, Lois safe. Only Maeve gone, now.

"Desmond and I are about to discuss . . . what the plot of this particular book is, I don't imagine it will take very long, I'll be home soon."

EIGHT

Controlling the instinct for recoil, savage rejection, she moved carefully out of his arms, which now held her lightly, as though he had gone away somewhere, leaving his body behind.

"*What* damned fools, Desmond?"

She realized later that her open exploration of the matter, her reading of the spreading ripples in the pond—so free, so candid—was a product of shock.

And she was wholly absorbed, fascinated, in what lay immediately before her eyes; not what loomed immensely, over and above and beyond.

"You sound so possessive about them—is it your Blessed Union behind all this? I never did believe in the I.R.A. theory anyway—it didn't have quite the right scent. And you on the sidelines, waiting and watching to see what happened—"

Desmond never stood on sidelines.

This too must be part of Desmond's new Michael Bye, and the task was to find out how she fitted into it, and Fen.

He had, while she talked, her voice soft and musing in the

quiet room, come back from wherever he had gone to.

"That was my last Val St. Lambert tumbler," he said, eyeing the glittering mess of broken crystal on the floor in front of the bookshelves. "And the end of the whiskey. A grand gesture, but an expensive one in every way. Ah, well. As a race, we're given to expensive gestures."

He went into the small kitchen at the far side of the round dining table and came out with a pilsner glass and a bottle of Guinness, which he poured with a steady hand. Apart from a high and handsome color under the gilded skin and the freckles, a special shimmer and shine to the blue of his eyes, he looked thoroughly himself.

"Sit down, Maeve, love, we've just begun our afternoon together. Sorry about the rude interruption to my music. Now where were we, you were threatening me about the Union, when—as for my overreaction, I happen to be on *their* side, whoever it was seized Gaymere and wants a chunk of his money. I'd like to have seen the whole thing go through cleanly. I heard this morning they were going to free those men, O'Toole and Quaid, everything laid on, jet, crew, it was going to happen sometime tonight. . . ."

He sat down in the leather chair close to where she sat, at the end of his sofa; he bent toward her, watching her face with the greatest interest.

"I forgot to ask you if you'd like a Guinness—"

"No . . ." The flowers and fruit and music, the wine and courting that had, in the end, torn her out of Fen's arms; she had come here to put a stop to these, and now there were other chapters in the same story that had to be dealt with. Before life, and love, and peace, and safety could be resumed.

"Brenda's house—oh, well, Mrs. Locket, of course," she said slowly. "You'd know the house is more or less closed up and she'd do anything for you, anything at all. I do think she'd balk at murder, but then, she wouldn't have to know that would be the end of it—and she'd think, you'd of course tell her—that it was for the cause, her cause. She's a fierce patriot, but she's a respectable woman and a snob too, she'd never willingly let a pack of strangers take over that house, take her over, order her about. But she would do it, and gladly, for you."

"Amuse yourself, Maeve," he said. "Continue with what you call your Michael Bye plot. Although I must say, professionally, that I'm better, quicker, at this kind of work than you are. But then, it's my living."

Under severe physical and emotional pressures which she was not entirely aware of her instincts kindled; her mind took a great leap.

"Lois—"

"Lois who?" He sipped Guinness.

"Lois Gaymere. You're the man who was, is, her lover—I thought it was impossible even when I found your cigarette holder, but then I had the wildest idea that you might want to move into my marriage, get at his family in some kind of revenge—"

After a short silence, he said, "What was that about the cigarette holder?"

"Your silver one. In a pencil cup in Lois's bedroom."

"I had no idea where I'd mislaid it—d'you happen to have it on you?" His self-possession took her a little aback. Perhaps he was right, that he was better and more professional, more believable, about this sort of work than she was. Perhaps her story was full of holes and would never bear the light of day. Well, get through one last, unlikely chapter, about him, and then maybe she had better abandon it, go back to her immediate business of bludgeoning him with the Blessed Union, get his agreement to cease and desist; and go home, to Fen.

He could, after all, have been violently sympathetic with a kidnapping that had nothing whatever to do with him.

But would he stop, would he ever stop? Love darling, D. —a goddamned bore—

She found a desperate concentration in herself.

Lois.

The extremes of secrecy about the identity of the man, even with her brother, to whom she was obviously close.

"Lover, wife, husband . . ." She held up three long fingers. "Money, a perfect ton of it." She added her little finger to the grouping. "And he was to be murdered . . ."

She could hear the bubbles winking out, one by one, in the quarter inch of light brown foam that topped his Guinness.

". . . and, if, in time, you married her, there would be nothing whatever to connect you with the period, we'll say months back, when she lost her husband." She was finding it a little difficult to breathe. "You were madly and hopelessly pursuing one Maeve Vaughan, whom you had loved on and off for years. Openly pursuing . . . showering presents . . . enraging her husband . . . up to and including a quarrel which is now no doubt on the police blotter, whatever *that* is. . . ."

He smiled at her. His high color had gone. "Too bad you've been seized from me by Vaughan, we might have collaborated nicely, you could have taken over when my invention broke down. The writing's easy, strawberries and cream, but let's face it, the plots are hell."

One final attempt; like trying with a bare and tender foot to kick down an iron door.

"I have been your alibi"—her lips lifted a little, fastidiously, away from the word—"all along. Even this afternoon, Edwin in Dublin, arrangements probably going on about Lois, I'm here with you—no wonder you were glad to see me, I couldn't understand it—you're free and clear of the matter, you even have a tape, I think, that says so—"

"I might use it at that, some time, your outline," he said. "Now that you've unburdened yourself of your dramatic imaginings, let's go back to practical matters." He added appreciatively, "However, I did enjoy your performance. You were talking very slowly, as though you were under hypnosis, or guided by the Holy Spirit, or something. Most effective. By the way, you left out the car bombing at Gaymere House."

She made an impatient gesture with her hand; the flicking away of a gnat.

"That's easy, Desmond. Stage a bombing, shatter some glass, and you brainwash everybody, including the police, into thinking whatever follows is political and not personal. A group, not a man. They—not 'he.' "

He threw back his head and laughed; a balloon-pricking, sane sound.

"My sweet Byzantine Maeve . . . wouldn't you after all like a drink? You look a bit frail suddenly."

She felt flattened and very tired. She hadn't had much sleep last night and now she was beginning to miss it.

Her voice for the moment casual with the sense of anticlimax, unreality, she asked, "Then . . . why did you put your arms around me like a kindhearted and unwilling executioner? And say, 'You didn't hear that, it wouldn't do for you to have heard that, not after—' "

"Because someone I know is a good friend of Quaid's, and I thought he might have something to do with this, he swore he'd get Quaid out, hell or high water. And I didn't want the police on my heels, trying to get me to help hound him down. Not that, on second thought, I think you'd quote me to the police. To repeat my own dangling words, not after—"

The day had changed. Rain swept the panes and the lamps bloomed brighter.

"Which brings us full circle, Desmond," she said. "Will you stop it, stop it at once, what you're doing to me? Not that I think your Blessed Union has much of a future, even if we make our bargain. . . . I suspect its sun has set, with the police poking about."

She yawned. The yawn reminded her that she mustn't relax, stop thinking. There was something wrong with the mood in this rain-echoing room. He had been close to a counterthreat when the news about Edwin Gaymere had sliced into the center of the symphony.

Now he was regarding her with a kind of gentleness, and sympathy. Did he think she was in for all kinds of terrible trouble with Fen?

"All right, a bargain, your word," he said. He looked at his watch. "Only one string to it. You will have a drink, and we will be friends, and civilized together, one last time. We will listen to music, and I will sit beside you and have a final immersion in your scent. And then I will take you home, Kathleen."

"Our business is over and I'm perfectly able to take myself home, right now."

He got up from the leather chair and stood over her, large, tall. She didn't know where the sense of imminent danger came from; he was still faintly smiling.

"Have a heart, darling. All those years. You're happy, very much in love, I gather. I happen to be standing at a graveside in the rain. I've lost the only person I ever wanted. The best part of my life is closed up in that big silver-handled box. . . ."

She was horrified at the tears in his eyes.

"For God's sake stop being Irish at me, Desmond. I know the words and the music too, remember? Don't sound so full of doom. You're a beautiful man and a clever one who can have anything and everything, if you'll only behave yourself."

In a way, it was reassuring to be scolding him; she had a lightheaded feeling of having come unscathed through what might have been a swamp full of alligators. If anything she had told him about himself, about what he might have been up to, had been true, she had been offering to him a very vulnerable neck.

Desmond Byrne, Michael Bye, would probably have a gun around somewhere, and certainly knew, at least on paper, how to use a knife, to say nothing of his bare hands.

But here he was, wanting only that she have a drink with him, take a short quiet walk into the past until he took her home, Kathleen.

"All right, as a matter of fact I am thirsty," she said. What, after all, was another little while? Let him talk, and she would just rest, and listen to his record he had just put on, Lili Kraus playing Mozart piano concertos.

Going back to the kitchen, he said over his shoulder, "As noted, the whiskey is all gone, but I happen to have a very cold bottle of champagne, will that do? Have you had any food, by the way, during your pursuit of me? Some crackers and cheese for you?"

"No, I'm not hungry, thank you."

Strange to be so formal with him; so polite. There was a loud festive pop from the kitchen. He came back with two filled tulip glasses. She took a small sip and noticed her hand was trembling a little and wondered why.

He sat close to her on the sofa. He made no attempt to touch her. He lifted his glass.

"To your new life, love, without hide nor hair of me."

She tried to smile back, to be pleasant, to be graceful about it, this little meaningless scrap of time out of her lovely freshly married life.

But she was tormented by the thought of Fen, wondering what she was doing here, why she was taking so long about it. She's safe in my arms, Vaughan. . . .

Desmond had fallen silent, not usual with him, and was looking at her in a leave-taking way she found uncomfortable. Nervously, she lifted her glass and drank more champagne.

The Lili Kraus record dropped. A rich and marvelous long-ago voice—McCormack—began.

*   *   *

The young may moon is beaming, love
The glowworm's lamp is gleaming, love
How sweet to rove through Morna's Grove
When the drowsy world is dreaming, love

Then awake, the heavens look bright, my dear
Tis never too late for delight, my dear
And the best of all ways to lengthen our days
Is to steal a few hours from the night, my dear

He bent and lightly kissed her mouth. "That's what I first kissed you to, remember?"

She had had enough. She said, "I must be off, now, Desmond."

"All right. I'll go out and get the car and bring it to the door. It would take us a week and a half to get a taxi on Caudle Street, in the rain."

"You needn't bother, really, I can—"

"Let's do it my way, on this closing anniversary. But first, do me a favor. Call your husband, I don't want him on the doorstep when I deliver you. For a literary man, he's very quick with his fist. Tell him you'll meet him at the Spread Eagle at a little after six, that you may be delayed but that in any case you won't be later than seven."

She didn't like or understand this at all.

"Why be so complicated about it? You can just drop me off, not that that's at all necessary but you seem to be insisting on it—"

"I said, let's do it my way." He took her hand and she thought deliberately hurt her by the savage tightening of his fingers. "I told you before you were here alone with me, there's nobody, nobody at all in this house but the two of us. You can think of yourself, dear girl, as my prisoner until you're inside your door."

Another of his moods; go along with it, anything to get home. But she disliked and rejected the idea of sending Fen, who might be anxious or furious or both, out into the rainy evening to meet her in a place she wouldn't be. More deception. More tricks and games played on him, by her and by Desmond.

She kept her face still, but her mind searched, as she walked over to the bamboo table that held the telephone, and dialed.

She was immediately answered.

How far she had come from the real world, this afternoon. Fen's voice jolted her, with its daylight ring of safety, reality.

"For Christ's sake, Maeve—where is my wandering girl now?"

Desmond had come to stand close beside her.

"About to jump into your arms, Fenway," she said. "Or as discreetly as that can be done, in public. I'm in too much of a hurry to explain, but will you meet me at the Spread Eagle, say a few minutes after six, I hope"—the words began to stick in her throat—"and at an outside chance, seven, at the latest."

A silence; he must be puzzling about the repeated, formal name, the oddness of the request after her long absence.

"Have a glass of Zaragosa waiting for me, will you, Fenway darling?"

She hoped, she prayed, he would get the message.

Elissa saying, "I think I'll have a glass of his own special sherry. No, not that bottle, the one behind it, I think I could find it in the dark—"

She had once used the words as a kind of weapon against him. His being able to know her mind, read between her lines, had been a recent discomfort. Now it might provide all the comfort in the world.

"The Zaragosa," Fen said slowly. "All right. Try not to be late."

No way of telling whether he knew, or didn't know, what she really meant.

Desmond made an impatient gesture.

"Good-bye then, see you soon."

He went to a closet and got out a black trench coat and a black umbrella.

"Wait here until I toot under the windows, no point in our both getting drenched. As a last domestic agreement between us, will you turn out the lights when you leave? I've an errand up your way, when you and I have said farewell, and I won't be back till late."

The door closed behind him.

She went directly to the telephone. A snatched golden opportunity to straighten things out with Fen, tell him to be there at the house in the mews.

Dial and dial again, into echoing silence. Out of order, perhaps . . . ? Or more probably, Desmond had flicked some kind of Michael Bye switch or adjustment on it.

After a very long ten minutes, waiting, she tried the front door knob, with an urgently rising temptation to flee. The door was locked. My prisoner, dear girl.

A moment later, unlocking noises. The door opened. "I did that out of habit," he said. "Come on, love. Home."

NINE

He was so tired that he came close to rejecting his deepest, surest instincts.

Zaragosa? She almost never drank sherry. He doubted very much the Spread Eagle could supply it; Alan Fort ordered it directly from Spain. "There's nothing quite like it, I don't know if you get the aftertaste of jasmine, my dear Fen . . ."

She wanted him home, for some reason, where this particular brand of sherry could be served. She also planned, verbally, to meet him at the Spread Eagle. The place dictated, probably, by Desmond, if she was still with Desmond.

Why the hours, the long hours, to say, Thank you, but I don't want any more violets or champagne?

Lafarge, the man who had died in a fog, in a car smash, against a tree. Had she made some bargain for his, Fen's life?

I'll cover you, protect you, hide you, give you an alibi, Desmond, for whatever you've done, whatever you've had to do, even with the Gaymeres, in exchange for—

Or perhaps she really wanted him away. The reference to

the sherry a reminder of his affair with Elissa. You, too, Fen, your slate isn't clean, either, we're both given to dallying, aren't we.

His body was raging at his enforced, inactive stay at the house in the mews, and longed to be moving, going somewhere. Why not the Spread Eagle? And then, if she didn't come after fifteen minutes, half an hour, back here to the house—

She hadn't sounded afraid; but she hadn't sounded happy or natural either.

Fenway.

Stay here, and see. It was not quite six. Mac gave him a pleading and expressive look. He leashed him and took him out into the heavy rain, up and down the mews, but not so far that he couldn't keep his eye on the door of Number 11.

When he got back, he shed his dripping raincoat and fed Mac and Doll, and then poured himself a drink. Four minutes after six. Would she be there now, waiting for him?

He called the Spread Eagle and asked if a Mrs. Fenway Vaughan was there.

"We're a bit noisy but I'll give her a hail," the friendly voice said. A minute later, "No one answering to that name, sir, we'll sing it out at intervals, shall she call you when she comes in? Let's have the number—"

He wished wearily that she had chosen another day, another time, to be mysterious with and about Desmond.

"Watch it, will you, Desmond?"

He had been driving too close on the heels of a white Rolls Royce which braked for the right turning into Millbank after the bridge had been crossed.

"Sorry. This rain is out to blind me—get me a cigarette, will you, Maeve? There's a packet in the glove compartment."

She flicked it open and stared at the gun, small, businesslike, resting on maps.

"The gun compartment, you mean," she said.

He took a fraction of a second from the traffic, the rain-bouncing street, to glance at her.

"I always keep it in the car, in case there are any highwaymen about. Here, if it makes you nervous—" He reached across her, put his hand into the compartment, reached over the gun, and took out the cigarettes.

"Light it for me . . . I'm collecting last times. Last time in

a car with you, last cigarette with a touch of your lipstick to
flavor it . . ." He was looking straight ahead of him. His voice
sounded strange. Was he entirely sober? He had had the champagne, and the Guinness, and she had no idea how many
scotches before she knocked on his door.

He drove, however, with his usual skill. After the deliberate
leisure he had insisted on, at his flat, he now seemed in a hurry.
Turning into the Vauxhall Bridge Road, he said, "I seem to
remember Fort has a garden. Is there a back way into the house?"

"Yes, why?"

"My dear innocent. After the news about Gaymere, and
Brenda's house, you may well have police waiting in front,
for you, and I have no desire, either, to encounter them."

"I forget the name of the street, but it's just north of the
mews . . ."

If Fen was in the house, as she hoped, as she had tried to
signal him to be, would Desmond then be walking unaware
into a nest of policemen? Because of course Fen would let
them in, he had nothing to hide, nothing to explain away.

She made a last effort. "Do, please, just drop me, Desmond,
at the back if you like, you may be right about the police—"

"I told you," he said. "I'm collecting last times. I'll want a
few minutes with you, out of this bloody rain, rain is not the
thing to say good-bye in."

There was no parking place beside the ivied brick garden
wall on the quiet street. He found one farther up. He reached
to open her door for her, and as she got out she saw him take
the gun out of the glove compartment and shove it into his
trench-coat pocket. He slid out and slammed his door, leaving
the car unlocked, opened his umbrella, and held it close over
the two of them. He clasped her arm firmly.

"Pick up your feet, love, the North Sea's upon us—"

"Why the gun, Desmond?"

"In case I meet with unexpected company."

Unexpected company? Fen.

Or perhaps the police—

The green garden door opened to her key. They went up the
path under dark dripping gingkos and plane trees. She tried the
handle of the back door, giving it a wrench to the right, hoping
it would make a noise, inside. Locked. She found the right
key, and unlocked it. The gun, the rain, the silent garden.

Unexpected company. For the first time with Desmond, she felt herself flooded from head to foot with terror.

The last of the Zaragosa in the drawing-room cabinet had been consumed.

He had just gone into the pantry to the left of the kitchen door when he heard the key in the lock and the door opening. Reaching for the light switch, his hand instinctively dropped.

The *back way?*

Her voice, near him, sweet and strangely level; a voice of which he knew every shading, this time walking delicately on eggs. And projected, as though to be heard a room or so away.

"Poor Fenway, waiting with my sherry at the Spread Eagle, a dirty trick—but in any case we can have a final toast. . . . How many of *those* have we had, darling, Dublin, Paris, New York. Hello, Mac, you remember Desmond—"

There was a rippling noise as someone's coat was stripped off.

"Pardon me while I make a dash to the front windows to see if they're out there," Desmond said, his voice already in the dining room.

Mac plunged into the pantry, lovingly. There was no light on in the kitchen. Maeve appeared, a dim shadow, and sensed rather than saw Fen. Her palm lifted to shoulder height and came strongly forward, at him. Back, Fen, back, it said. Turning, she pulled the swinging door to.

Nothing to operate on now, but some kind of personal Morse code, straining to interpret its dots and dashes, second to second.

Mac put a cold nose into his hand, in the dark.   .

She was, he thought, very frightened, for some reason; but concealing it well, except from his exactly receiving ears. And she didn't want him seen. Not yet. Not this particular second.

"Sit, Mac," he whispered. "Stay."

He opened the pantry door again, into the dark kitchen. He latched it on Mac.

". . . not a soul," he heard Desmond say. A carrying voice, a note higher than he remembered it. "Unless that's a Scotland Yard cat huddled in the doorstep across the street—a final toast, you said?"

"Yes, will you fix it, everything's in the cabinet there—"

He moved through the kitchen and into the unlighted dining

room, alert, waiting, neither hiding nor showing himself. He thought it would be a good thing to know, cleanly and finally and forever, about Maeve and Desmond.

What was it she didn't want him to see, to hear, to be exposed to, with Desmond in the house, thinking himself to be alone with her?

The lamps in the hall had not been turned on but light from the drawing room touched the far dining-room walls faintly. Clinking noises, a bottle against another bottle.

"Do hurry, Desmond darling, I want a bath and a rest, last night was a bit rough, and he'll be back soon, which will make an affectionate good-bye a little awkward—"

"We have until seven, if he's the reliable sort he looks, but perhaps you're right . . ."

Crystal to crystal; a thin high ring.

"All the same," he said on a long sigh, "I do think it was a lovely plot of yours, Maeve, that you worked out. I in the bosom of your family, so to speak, face to face with your Vaughan, for the rest of our lives, rich and happy I'd be, to boot—she's not you, the sister, but she'll do—would have, rather—"

Bitterness rose in the listening man in the dining room and caught in his throat. Was this the bargain she had made? Lois, widowed Lois, in payment for her own husband?

Or had there been no bargain at all, just something she was doing for her Desmond, or helping him to do for himself. Of course you can use Brenda's house, darling—

No wonder she had wanted him out of hearing, in the pantry.

A farewell; and two who had been lovers taking leave of a failed, ruined plan.

But why, then, had she wanted him in the house at all? For a black moment, he thought, *Who cares*. He had been so sure he knew her and known he loved her, but now—

"Yes, might as well get this down and be off, a jealous husband is a terrible thing, Maeve."

Her voice, still light: "You were no help in that department, Desmond."

A sudden sense of motion from the room beyond.

A sound to stop the heart, half choke, half scream, from Maeve, the other voice winded, hoarse with pain, or passion.

"Didn't you know you got it all in one, back there—at the flat . . . You know me too well—oh love oh love, I'm sorry—"

Fen moved.

Desmond, standing on the hearthrug, where he had once kissed her, body embracing hers; now, too, embracing. Elbows high, head bent lovingly over her shoulder to his task, he was strangling Maeve.

A dream repeated. Tearing the powerful flesh and bone from his wife. But this time they both went down together and Maeve made a strange harsh noise and stumbled and fell across her husband's legs.

He had one arm around her and had half flung himself upright when he was caught with a frightful blow on the side of his head from Desmond's balled and murderous fist.

He saw the face up close, in obscene intimacy, the golden hair tossed, a suffusion of red purple under the skin, teeth showing, even the blue eyes with a reddish glare to the whites. Tears streaked and stained the freckled cheekbones.

Desmond rolled free, watching in turn the stunned strong pale face, flung back on the neck, fighting unconsciousness, then lifting again, the arm still clasping Maeve; she had fainted.

He got up and delivered a cruel and insulting kick to the ribs and watched the back arch with pain.

"It's your turn now for the hearthrug, Vaughan," he said, reaching for the coat tossed over the back of the sofa, and taking from a pocket his gun.

He half-leaned against the sofa, gun held firmly, its muzzle pointing directly at Fen's face. Fen had managed to raise himself on his elbow. Maeve was a warm, crippling heap over his lower body.

Very delicately, Desmond shifted the direction of the gun, toward Maeve's head. She was face down, shining hair spilled over Fen's outflung palm.

He felt her heart, beating against his thigh. Alive, alive-o, he thought, his mind working, recording, in some remote place, but —

"I'd wanted it neat," Desmond said, slowly and carefully. "Just her. We've known each other too long and too well. And you of course the culprit, they always look to the mate first, as I told her a few minutes ago, a jealous husband is a terrible thing. . . ."

Watching with a sense of ice and finality the motion of the gun, from his own head to Maeve's, his eye caught the book he had been trying to read, centuries ago, waiting for Tom's call, waiting to hear where Maeve had gone when she left him. It was open, face down, on the edge of the galleried table inlaid with forget-me-nots.

His head was clearing. It thundered with pain, and he thought a rib or two might be broken. But there was no way he could move, now. And he had closed and latched the pantry door on Mac, so that his listening—and now, he thought, sickened— coldly suspicious presence in the dining room would not be heralded by the dog.

"You're in a most convenient topple there," Desmond went on. "And after she goes, my darling, my only love, well, you wouldn't want to live without her anyway, would you? . . . You probably don't descend to my kind of fiction, but the gun, you see, afterward, is placed in your hand. Wiped, of course, first. With the best Irish linen."

Ridiculously, amazingly, the doorbell rang.

Desmond jerked his head in its direction. Fen flung himself forward and upward in one great swift curve, lifted the book from the edge of the table, and aimed it with life or death accuracy. The spine struck Desmond's face, swiveling around again, hard and squarely between the eyes. It was a large and heavy book: Volume II of Greville's *Memoirs*. He went backward, over the sofa, like a tremendous upset doll. Fen, gently but instantly freeing himself of Maeve, got up, leaned over, and took the gun from his hand.

It went off changing hands and made a hole that Alan Fort afterward treasured and showed off to his guests, accompanied by its tale, in the copper gilt frame of the bull's-eye mirror over the mantelpiece.

Holding it, the first gun he had ever touched, watching Desmond dazedly rearranging himself, using his Irish linen not to wipe off fingerprints but to mop blood from his forehead and nose, Fen lifted Maeve, found that she was finally murmuring, and half-aware, and able to support herself, and with his eyes very steadily on Desmond moved to the hall, put an arm behind him, and turned the door handle.

Lois's voice said, "Is that all I get, Fen, your back? Maeve, what's the matter, is there something . . . ?"

In desperate command of himself, Fen said, "Stay here in the hall for a bit. Maeve, sit down. . . ."

He lowered her to the cane armchair beside the desk, watching Desmond through the door as he did so.

Lois looked over his shoulder, into the drawing room. Desmond had righted himself and was standing, on the hearthrug he had made so very much his own, dangerously still, bloodied handkerchief dangling from his hand.

"Ian, darling." Her voice was just a little above a whisper. She was very pale, and her dark blue linen suit was severely crumpled; but in the quick flick of a glance Fen allowed himself, she looked entirely unharmed.

"Don't go near him," Fen said. "You'd make a very nice bulletproof vest for him. He just tried to kill Maeve. I want the two of you upstairs, right away."

Taking him very much by surprise, Lois swept his gun hand down against his side.

"Run, darling, run!" she cried. "He won't shoot you in the back, he couldn't—he doesn't approve—"

Moving like lightning, Desmond spun around, reached one of the locked, long windows opening on the garden, hit it with a great crash of his shoulder. To the tinkle of falling glass, and the billowing of the curtains on the rainy air, and the faint patter as drops struck the parquet floor, he was gone.

Lois had her hands over her face, shoulders bent, dark hair falling forward, in an ancient posture of woe. Tears trickled through her fingers. Her shoulders shook.

"I don't at all understand, about Maeve, but I couldn't bear him in defeat—I won't, I can't remember him that way—"

Fen gave her a look, half-pitying and half-furious; and then said mildly, "You're right, I couldn't have shot him in the back," and went to the telephone and dialed the police.

TEN

"Perhaps you won't want me any longer, Fen."

The blue and white room was quiet. Maeve sat in her night-gown by the fire. It was lit, and the flames were playing vigorously, over the sighs and crackles of wood, but she was shivering.

He went to the closet and got her green robe and lifted her from the chair.

"Put this on."

She had told him about the Michael Bye story she had laid before Desmond at the flat on Caudle Street. The awful danger of what she had been doing still froze him.

But then, she had felt some kind of immemorial safety; she had thought that he would never hurt her, no matter what.

Almost impossible pellet to swallow, even now: it was he, Fen, who was to have killed her. "A jealous husband is a terrible thing. . . ."

And if she hadn't had the wit to put two syllables to his name, and ask for the sherry Elissa had liked to drink at Alan

Fort's, after moving from his own arms—"Put it on the edge of the tub, darling—"

If she hadn't done these things, Desmond's plan would have worked, efficiently and well.

He would have come back at a little after seven, from the Spread Eagle, angry, frustrated, and found her body, which would still have been warm, soft, spilled in final disaster. There would be no curious residents of the mews with stories of a black car in front of the coral-painted door, a man going into Number 11 with her; because they had come in at the back, nothing to be seen but two figures in the lash of rain, obviously unidentifiable under a great black umbrella.

He had at first thought it a rather baroque gesture on Desmond's part, the killing of Maeve in her own quarters; but on chilled reflection he realized that it had been merely practical.

If she had been poor, obscure, or both, an undermanned police force might have taken considerable time to cope with the discovered dead body; to find out why and under what circumstances and where the red-haired young woman had died.

But she was attractive and well-dressed and well-bred, the wife of an American visitor; there was money to add flavor to the story, his money and Brenda's. And the Gaymere kidnapping and Trann's murder to bring it not only to the front pages of the newspapers but right up on top, in headlines.

Disposing of the body would be awkward, after he had killed her in the privacy of the Caudle Street flat. What to do with her? The Thames? Some rank alley in Soho? But no, the news would be out that she was missing, the police radios would be blaring—

Much better to attach the body, and the blame, to the usual first-choice candidate: the husband.

He had informed the police, when they were wanting to talk to Maeve, that he had no idea where she was, that they had had a fight.

And she had passed the marvelously convenient quarrel to Desmond, in the course of explaining to him exactly what he had been up to. He would have known by this time that she couldn't be allowed to live, not possibly. Beloved by him, she might be, but the end of his world.

He looked in a sort of exhausted wondering joy at the woman in the green robe, head bent, hair falling, with the firelight stroking it.

He heard her going on, remotely, "It turns out I'm not your style at all, Fenway and Vaughan, East Thirty-eighth Street. It was just sheer luck that you haven't, through me, a dead brother-in-law as a sort of post wedding present—"

"But he isn't dead, he's alive and probably already investing in something." He was surprised to hear that his own voice sounded as far away as hers did. "And Lois—you can't hold yourself responsible for that chapter of his. You didn't throw her into his arms. A woman does this on her own, for her own reasons. If she hadn't, his plans would have gotten nowhere. Poor Lois—"

Lois hadn't wanted to leave Number 11 Polperry Mews. "Edwin will be holding conferences, board meetings, with the police, and I don't think I can face it, can I stay here? And will you call him and tell him, say I'm ill and in shock and can't see anybody until tomorrow morning, when I'll let the police debrief me, or whatever they do—"

He removed Alan Fort's sleeping pills and what he suspected were his tranquilizers, little blue tablets, "Two a day if needed for stress," from the medicine cabinet in Alan's bathroom, after he had pulled up the taffeta puff over Lois and kissed her. He closed the door to the sound of her soft weeping, beginning again.

Now, at the forlorn statements from the fireside, he went over and lifted Maeve again from her chair and held her. She had stopped shivering. She buried her face against him.

"Do I want you any longer? For the rest of our lives—as soon as you've stopped mourning Desmond."

She lifted her head. Her eyes raged, green, a few inches under his. "*Mourning!* An executioner, standing aloof, giving the orders, having his Blessed Union men do the dirty work, Edwin to go, Trann killed, and then your idiot wife, facing him with her story, his story—and you to be held accountable, you to have killed me with your hands, your hands that I love—"

A lone police car had spotted Michael Bye's plates as the black Jaguar went down a slanting cement drive in Pimlico, between a long-closed church and its abandoned rectory. Lois, trying to eat the broth Maeve had made for her, listening to the radio, said, "But that sounds—the cellars, and the brass bed, and the ivy growing over the church, that's where I was . . . and I thought I was in another country." She tried to take a half teaspoonful of broth. "I can see him stalking a cell, in prison, shaking the bars, like some beautiful golden thing trapped in Regent's Park Zoo—''

Brenda called from San Francisco on the heels of an alarming news bulletin, just after Fen had said, "Even this kind of day has to come to an end. Rise from your ashes, as you once said to him— Bed, darling."

It was Maeve who had to soothe Brenda; after she had told her the whole story, her aunt was in a state of considerable distress.

"I'm fine, a very sore throat, a rusty voice for a day or so—and Fen's right here." Comfort and love, a warm inch or so away, waiting.

"And Mrs. Locket, poor soul, will have to spend some time in prison, I suppose," Brenda sighed. "I imagine she fed him well, though, Gaymere, she can't cook a bad dish if she tries. I think I'm going to have to drop my theory about there being only so many people in the world—it's bad luck. To think it was your own cousin by marriage responsible for all this— Is your Fen angry at the Devlins and Delanoys and all their ilk?"

Fen, who had been listening, took the receiver from her hand. "No, Brenda, not at all. It works both ways, you know. You're my ilk too, now."

"What a dear boy you are to be sure," Brenda said. "See that she gets a decent sleep, Fen."

"I will," Fen promised.

"I think there must be some way I can get one of those elegant round blue enamel historical plaques mounted on this house," Alan Fort said. The headlines had been too much for him; he had come back from Italy several days earlier than he had expected.

"I mean, darlings, the scene of such derring-*do!* Stranglings and kidnappings—yes, I promise not to say anything about the strangling, just think, right over *there* by my sofa. Imagine anyone having the nerve to try and make off with Edwin Gaymere! Like stealing the Bank of England, pillar by pillar—"

He eagerly gobbled inside information, sipping his Zaragosa sherry.

"And the Blessed Union? One wishes that one had thought it up, so much easier than working away at the typewriter."

"In disarray," Fen said. "Byrne refused to supply the names of his minions, but they've got Cooley, from Maeve's description of him, and Cooley's not being in the least heroic about his associates. I don't think any more contributions will be coming in."

"Did the first, original threats on Gaymere's life come from Byrne too?"

"No, they were apparently authentic—he just moved in and took over. It was all very conveniently set up for him."

"Such an extremely attractive rogue," Alan Fort murmured, with a thoughtful glance at Maeve. "His pictures—amazing. I would like to know the name of his tailor. How will he bear being . . . incarcerated?"

"Better than most, I imagine," Maeve said, in a voice her husband was happy to hear was objective and healthily calm. "As long as there's something to look forward to, morning tea to drink, and the next cigarette, and something to be turned to his advantage—just wait, we'll see how that goes—Desmond will cherish his life, every minute of it."

The press had a marvelous time with Desmond, whom a woman journalist christened the "Thriller Killer." He was, as Maeve had pointed out to him, frightfully photogenic, and always superbly dressed. His dignity and grace were unshakable throughout. During the pretrial period, he received in the mail forty-nine proposals of marriage from women all over the world, in case he should get off.

At Maeve's impassioned request—"Please, or we'll have to come back here for the trial, don't say anything to the police about his trying to kill me, there's enough to put him away properly for a long, long time. I don't want to be there on the witness stand, spading the earth for the grave—yes, Fen, Irish overstatement, I know—but, please—" Fen kept the matter of the attempted murder of his wife more or less a family secret.

From Princetown Prison, Michael Bye wrote two books a year. His only work of nonfiction, *The Gaymere Tale*, was made into a major motion picture.